CHUTES AND LADDER

CHUTES AND LADDER

A Silicon Valley Mystery

Marc Jedel

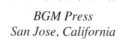

BGM Press
San Jose, California

Published in the United States by BGM Press.

ISBN 978-1-7327164-1-4 (paperback edition)

Cover designed by Alchemy Book Covers

Sign up for my mailing list to receive free content, learn of new releases, and receive special offers:

http://www.marcjedel.com

1

Friday Afternoon

"What do you call a fly without wings?" No response, so I answered my own joke. "A walk."

I watched the kid for a reaction. I didn't know him, but he was stuck watching my niece's soccer game next to me. He popped another Goldfish cracker into his mouth without comment. Three-year-olds didn't get my sense of humor. Appreciation for that level of advanced wit didn't begin until age five.

My sister, Laney, sitting on my other side, made a disgusted sound. "That's it. I'm going for a run."

"Wait, is it over?" I started gathering my things as hope spread throughout my stiff body.

Laney snorted. "No, silly. It's halftime. They'll eat oranges for fifteen minutes while the coach gives them instructions they won't follow. I'll be back." She stood up from the grass, did a quick stretch, and jogged off around the fields.

She didn't appreciate my jokes either, which wasn't exactly a news flash to me. I'd seen more of Laney in the last few months since her move to the Bay Area than I had since we were kids.

Although we'd aged, my sense of humor, like most men, remained firmly rooted at the childhood level.

The kid wandered off too, no doubt looking for something he found more exciting than me—like the clods of dirt he started kicking. My niece, Skye, played defensive stopper for her eighth-grade rec league team, meaning she hung around talking to the goalie and the other defenders on her team while the action took place at the other end of the field. I wasn't too clear on why I had to be there—something about an important game that would determine who played in the upcoming championship. The league moved this match up by a day because many of the girls would be out of town on Saturday at a Girl Scout campout.

The outcome of this game had no meaningful impact. The first-place team would receive cheap metal-and-plastic trophies at a pizza parlor to celebrate their all-important victory. All the other teams would also receive cheap metal-and-plastic trophies at other pizza parlors to console them for not finishing first. Skye had asked me to come watch, and she did say "pretty please."

As a result, here I sat on a warm, late October afternoon, without even an appreciative audience for my humor, while my software code wasn't writing itself. I closed my eyes, at least enjoying the rare opportunity to sit outside in the daylight during the week.

Off in the distance, Laney rounded the corner of another soccer field. I watched the coach haranguing the girls for a while and tried to figure out why this sport had become so popular. The game resembled kickball in front of one or the other team's net. It had none of the strategy and excitement of a real sport, like baseball.

Okay, maybe baseball didn't have much action, but the ballparks did serve beer.

When I looked back toward the other field, Laney was no longer in sight. Had she gone supersonic to get some coffee before halftime ended?

Confused, I stood up, cupping a hand over my eyes to block

the glare of the setting sun, and spotted Laney lying prone on the ground by the empty field. I jogged toward her—actually, it became more of a lumbering fast walk when my huffing and puffing made me realize that avoiding the gym hadn't improved my endurance.

Laney was holding her ankle and fighting back tears when I reached her. "What happened?"

"Help me up," she responded, wincing as she got to her hands and knees.

I complied. "Strange place to take a nap," I said, trying to distract her from the pain.

"Stupid animals. Digging stupid holes." She flicked a dismissive hand at the offending hole in the ground that had tripped her.

Laney put her arm around my shoulders and hopped back to the stands, muttering and cursing in a low voice.

"Does it hurt that much?" I asked.

"I've got to take Skye to the campout tomorrow morning. I just hope they can give me something for the pain so it's better by tonight."

For Skye's sake, I hoped so too. Camping wasn't my cup of tea, but I'd hate for her to miss out. It wasn't that I didn't like nature. Nature was great. Living in the Bay Area meant that I went hiking on a regular basis. With the help of my new friend, Brody, a barista at a nearby Starbucks, I'd even rekindled my love of the ocean. At the ripe age of forty, surfing hurt my knees too much, so I went kayaking with him instead.

Camping was a different story. After the campfire petered out for the evening and the songs were sung, I held to the unpopular belief that people and nature should retire to their own separate quarters. People lived inside and nature belonged outdoors, along with all its affiliated bugs, animals, and whatever else went bump in the dark.

By the time I'd half-carried Laney back to our chairs, I was drenched in sweat. I'd have picked her up, but she was a grown woman… not to mention that gym thing again.

Despite the periodic whimper or curse from Laney, she refused to leave until the game ended. Although we could have asked another parent to bring Skye home, she wanted to tough it out to support Skye and her team. Since her husband died a few years ago, Laney always tried to go the extra mile for her girls.

Out of respect for her pain and sacrifice, I only cracked a few more jokes during the second half.

We hobbled out of there to head for the hospital as soon as the game ended. And the handshake line with the defeated team. And the celebratory run through the parents' tunnel of raised arms. And the hug with each teammate. And the snatching of the postgame snack of cupcakes. *Score!*

I would have to drive Laney's rental car to the hospital so she could have her ankle X-rayed. Despite my offer of a steep family discount, she refused to use Rover, the startup self-driving car service where I worked as a software engineer. We ran one of those next-generation car services that transported people without a driver. Our marketing team thought Rover was a catchy name because the cars fetched passengers whenever they needed a ride, but I always had to explain it. People weren't newspapers and cars weren't dogs. Besides, who reads a newspaper these days? At least we had a great engineering team, even if the marketing folks were only so-so.

Laney was either old-fashioned or didn't trust my engineering skills. I preferred not to find out which was the case.

Her last car had been totaled a month ago in a bad accident involving an ice cream truck and a drone. Not to brag or anything, but I basically saved her life and helped put a really bad person behind bars for a long time. Just another average day in the life of wannabe super-secret agent, Marty Golden.

Okay, I got lucky.

I sure didn't miss Laney's "Sunshine," a Beetle with a custom neon-yellow paint job. It might have even glowed in the dark. Ever since the accident, Laney and her girls had spent a ridiculous amount of time trying to decide on her next Beetle's custom paint job. I could only hope her new color choice wouldn't be so painful on the eyes.

As Laney and I reached the car, Skye finished gossiping with her teammates and joined us. She was my oldest niece, a pretty twelve-year-old with long hair pulled back in a ponytail to keep it out of her eyes while she played. Like Superman reverting back into Clark Kent, she'd put her glasses back on after the game, resuming her appearance as a serious future scientist. "Mom, what made you fall?" she asked.

"I think a rabbit or a gopher startled me, and I stepped into a hole," said Laney.

Skye shut the car door behind her. "It's okay to tell Megan, right?" Skye's younger sister had traveled to Portland for a long weekend visit with their cousins.

Megan was a lively sparkplug of a girl. She was seven. Or eight. Nine at the most. Definitely somewhere in that range. I was embarrassed that I didn't know, but when I tried to ask, they all made fun of me and didn't answer.

At Laney's nod, Skye turned her focus to her phone and texted the latest update to her sister.

As I pulled out of the parking lot, I felt the need to one-up Laney. "You got tripped up by a silly rabbit? We'll have to start calling you Alice."

When there was no response from the backseat, I glanced in the mirror. "Hey, Skye!"

Trying to catch the attention of a pre-teen with her nose buried in her phone was like pulling teeth. But I persevered. "Did I ever tell you that, in college, we used to have a scary monster goose that hung around the pond in the middle of campus? It would attack kids who walked past. Everyone called it 'Triceragoose.'"

Skye snorted. Unlike three-year-olds, pre-teens appreciated my stories.

Laney didn't give up a competition that easily. "Goose schmoose. We had this huge deer that hung around my campus. One day I was walking to the shuttle bus stop and the deer stepped out of the woods and blocked the road. It stared down the bus, so the bus driver had to pick us up half a block back and do a U-turn."

I scoffed. "Huge deer. Did you call it Rudolph or Bambi?" As we ran over one of San Jose's endless potholes, I saw Laney wince in pain, so I stopped teasing her.

Skye noticed too and patted her mom's shoulder before returning her attention to her phone.

*****

Despite Laney returning to the hospital only a month after her last stay, the nurses and doctors still treated her like all their other patients. By the time her ankle had been X-rayed, braced and booted, and we got back to her house, we were all cranky.

Skye and I grabbed some leftover chicken and salad from the refrigerator. "Did Nurse Ruth give you laughing gas in the hospital?" I asked Laney. "What were you laughing about?"

I'd met Nurse Ruth when Laney was hurt last month. Although she'd taken good care of Laney, I'd tricked her into letting an underage visitor, my niece Megan, into Laney's room after visiting hours and then abused her trust. So, basically, we were buds.

From her seat at the kitchen table, Laney chuckled. "Nurse Ruth asked if you had hurt me."

"Me?" Shocked, I stopped dead in my tracks. Why would I hurt my sister? Maybe we hadn't always gotten along well as kids, but we were older now.

Laney shifted her glance to the large Labrador puppy that wandered around the kitchen without helping Skye and me get dinner on the table. "I told her the only time you've caused me pain since I moved to town was when you got us a crazy dog who almost destroyed my house."

My mouth suddenly dry, I licked my lips. "Well, Megan shouldn't have left her Adderall pill out where Buddy could reach it."

Laney's eyes flashed. "Don't blame her. That dog tore up papers all over the house. He was bouncing off the walls, grabbing and chewing things, and peeing everywhere. It cost me a thousand dollars for the pet hospital to pump his stomach."

Before I could respond, Skye burst out laughing. "It was so gross and so hysterical. He kept running in circles until he, like, collapsed."

I managed to stifle my smile. Laney was still unhappy with me for surprising the girls with the dog last month. "Well, the crate should help." I tilted my head toward the large dog crate that took up much of the available kitchen space.

Eyes still smoldering at Buddy, Laney didn't look like she appreciated the crate any more than the dog.

Yeah, Buddy was one of my more impulsive gifts, but it could have been worse—he could have been my dog.

"Your payback is taking Skye on her campout."

"What?" I was stunned. She knew I did not go camping.

"The doctor said I need to rest my foot if I'm going on that business trip next week. I can't tramp around the woods, so you'll have to man up and take Skye."

"Please, Uncle Marty …" Skye tilted her head to the side and tried her puppy-dog eyes on me.

She forgot I didn't like dogs. And I hated camping even more.

No way would I take Skye on her camping trip. Even though she and Laney had babbled on and on about this campout, I had to draw the line somewhere. For me, that line was drawn around a nice hotel room, with a door that closed, a shower, effective air conditioning, and a comfy bed.

"Oh, come on, it's only one night. Don't be a baby," Laney pushed, but I didn't budge.

"Pretty please." Skye tried her underhanded puppy-dog trick again before upping her game. "I'll laugh at all your jokes."

I gave the offer serious consideration. That could almost be worth it, but only if she'd convince her friends to laugh too. Then, I remembered all the other moms who would be there. They wouldn't laugh.

I used a second, better excuse. "I can't. I need to fly to Portland early on Monday morning, remember?" I was excited to see a major *Star Trek* exhibition at the Oregon Museum of Science and Industry and didn't want to jeopardize my trip. I'd wanted to go for the whole weekend to spend more time there, but I hadn't been able to convince my new girlfriend, Meghan, to go. Somehow, learning that it was the biggest *Star Trek* exhibition west of the Mississippi hadn't been enough to convince her. Our relationship was still new, and I was smart enough not to choose *Star Trek* over her or raise too many questions about her obvious lack of good judgment. So, I was reduced to a day trip to check out the show while she left for a business trip to the East Coast.

Laney shook her head in exasperation. "You and your silly *Star Trek* thing. The girls come home on Sunday afternoon, so you won't miss anything. Besides, I don't want you to miss your flight either. You're flying home with Megan from Portland on Monday afternoon, remember?"

I didn't know how she kept track of all these complicated comings and goings. One girl had Friday off school while the other had Monday off. One was off to the wilderness to fend for her life while the other had to pack the right gear for the Pacific Northwest rainforest. The following week would be even more complicated thanks to Laney's own business trip.

I had to resort to my final excuse. "I can't take your place. You have to be authorized to attend a Girl Scouts event as a chaperone." Last month, I had agreed to help out for a cookie table outside a Whole Foods grocery store, figuring I'd score some extra cookies when the girls weren't looking. One of the moms told me I had to leave because I hadn't registered as a volunteer in advance. To make matters worse, I had to buy my own cookies. No compensation for waking up early on a weekend.

The evil grin spreading over Laney's face made me worry. "Oh"—her voice rang in a high-pitched tone of glee—"you're registered now."

"What? I don't remember registering for anything!"

"I did it for you … just in case. You even passed the background check."

I did?

Laney looked triumphant before turning serious. "Besides, I can't go now, and Skye is required to have an adult chaperone." She paused. "Even you count."

My winning arguments had all flopped.

Laney had crushed my final, desperate attempt to avoid sleeping in the dangerous Santa Cruz Mountains, full of wild squirrels, insects, dirt, and trees. As eerie as Redwoods could be during the daytime, they were much more frightening in the dark.

I jerked back as Buddy startled me by wandering too close to my chair. Using my foot so I wouldn't have to touch anything furry or wet, I shoved him farther away.

Silence fell over the kitchen as I struggled to come up with another argument, but Skye filled the void with a whoop of excitement. "I'll get you a sleeping bag and the packing list." She flew off to her room as Buddy barked and ran after her, bouncing off the walls and knocking a few pictures askew. My jaw moved up and down a few times without any noise coming out.

Laney kept her mouth shut, her smug grin showing she was smart enough not to sell past the close.

Sighing and scratching my head led to no new inspiration. I wasn't a happy camper.

*****

Far too early on a Saturday morning, I found myself sitting in the Rover car with Skye as it turned into the Girl Scout Camp parking lot. The entrance sign way back at the highway exit announced that the newly merged and renovated Santa Cruz County Park and Girl Scout campsite had reopened earlier this year.

A woman with a hat pulled down low against the morning sun drove past us, heading back out to civilization. Pointing my thumb at her, I asked Skye, "Can't I just drop you off and leave like her?"

Skye's face clouded up. "Everyone has to have a chaperone." With a sly smile, she added, "Besides, we'll have s'mores tonight."

Now she was playing for keeps, and learning Laney's tricks all too quickly. Who didn't like marshmallows dripping with chocolate, smashed between two crunchy graham crackers? Maybe the crackers would even be cinnamon-flavored? Or there might be ice cream! Ice cream with s'mores sounded pretty good to me.

The Rover car let us out and left at a rapid clip. I didn't blame it for abandoning me. Perhaps I'd talk to Raj, my brilliant engineering coworker at Rover, about adding a feature to have Rover cars check that their passengers felt comfortable at the drop-off location before leaving. They might even sound two soft beeps for a friendly goodbye. Goodbye, good luck, and hope you survive your night in the wilderness.

Skye ran up to join the cluster of girls huddled around a picnic table stacked with backpacks and bags of supplies. The girls and other parents, all moms, buzzed with excitement as they pointed to the new facilities. The handful of concrete buildings and fire pits, a sand volleyball court, and the rough landscaping didn't look too impressive to me.

Everyone went silent when I set my backpack, supplies, and sleeping bag on the table. The moms, with Starbucks cups held high, paused their conversations and shot me looks ranging from skeptical to downright hostile.

One mom, with curly red hair exploding around her face and wearing a lightweight puffy jacket, gave me a warm welcome. "What are you doing here? You can't stay. This is a Girl Scouts campout." She emphasized the word "girl" as if I hadn't noticed my surroundings and had gotten lost in the woods.

Before I could answer, a shrill whistle sounded. We all turned to see an older woman striding toward us from one of the concrete buildings. She had shoulder-length, straight gray hair under a ball cap with "B.A.W.S.I." stenciled on the front. Over cargo shorts, she wore a blue hoodie with the arms cut off like that NFL head coach of the New England Patriots who won all those Super Bowls. The sweatshirt had a white logo for Notre Dame San Jose, a private all-girls high school. Her whistle hung on an orange cord around her neck, ready for use again. When she reached us, she pulled on her green jacket vest crowded with Girl Scout badges and what appeared to be a dozen jammed pockets, buttoned or zipped, full of secret supplies.

Ignoring the others, she turned to me. "You must be Marty Golden," she said in a flat, rough voice.

"Yes." *How'd you guess?*

"Well, congratulations. I checked the system, and you have official clearance. You're Skye's chaperone for this trip." She didn't sound any more excited than I was. As her words sank in, the women gathered around us groaned.

She snapped, "Girl Scouts don't complain. It's my fault for not registering this trip as a women's-only overnight." She sighed. "We'll deal with it. Some of you will have to shift around so Mr. Golden can have his own tent."

More grumbling ensued. My popularity was soaring.

She blew her whistle again, deafening all of us. "Oh, and one more thing. The Council told me the bathroom plumbing isn't working yet. We'll have to use the 'biffy' this trip." This was met with the largest groan yet, but I didn't understand why.

What I did know was that we needed a whistle like that at Rover to get everyone focused on fixing serious bugs when our system crashed. Knowing how grumpy my boss got at times, though, such a powerful tool in his hands might not be such a great idea after all. I didn't believe he could handle that whole "with great power comes great responsibility" thing, even if that responsibility was just a Girl Scout whistle.

I didn't hear whatever else the troop leader told the others as her third whistle blow startled me out of my daydream. She shouted, "No more complaints. Let's get everything set up so we can start having fun. Remember, we have a schedule to keep." She clapped twice. The huddle broke, and everyone headed off as if executing a prearranged play.

I hadn't received my copy of the playbook and had missed the instructions. I stood there unmoving, not sure of my role in this setup effort. Skye, noticing my indecision, came over and introduced us. "Uncle Marty, this is my troop leader, Mrs. Payne."

Proud of Skye's politeness, I aimed to start off on a good foot with my leader for this weekend. Holding out my hand, I said, "Hi. How are you?"

"Busy," came Mrs. Payne's curt response. "Carry these supplies to the storeroom." She waved in the vague direction of the stuff around us and strode off with some of the other women.

Feeling a warm and fuzzy glow from the friendly welcome, I asked Skye, "Do you know what B.A.W.S.I. on her hat stands for? Is it some clever acronym for 'bossy?'"

"Ha, ha. That means Bay Area Women's Sports something," said Skye. "Mrs. Payne was a coach at Notre Dame High School before she retired."

That explained her whistle. I even remembered hearing of B.A.W.S.I. in some story about getting local girls excited to play sports. "So, what's a 'biffy,' and where is it?"

Skye laughed for real this time. "Silly! That's another acronym. It's Girl Scout speak for a 'Bathroom In The Forest For You'—B.I.F.F.Y. It's all around you." She swept her arms around, reminding me that trees, animals, and bugs surrounded our clearing. Then she skipped off after some of her friends, leaving me speechless and wondering if I could hold it in for a whole day.

Trying to fit in with the Girl Scouts team, I worked hard to show my value. I hustled to carry the supplies to the nearby building Mrs. Payne had exited earlier, which hadn't sounded like a complicated instruction. Yet, somehow, I screwed it up. How was I supposed to know that supplies didn't mean the backpacks? Or that the nearby building was the camp office rather than the storeroom? If Mrs. Payne wanted me to take only the bags of food into the building with the refrigerators, then she should have said so. Girl Scout campsites needed more signage and clearer instructions.

Rather than dwelling on mistakes, I've found it best to focus on the future. In the future, I planned to avoid Girl Scout events like the plague. Unless free cookies were involved.

After another misunderstanding of Mrs. Payne's instructions, I found myself standing by a firepit, hovering on the outskirts of the cluster of girls while listening to them sing different Girl

Scout songs. When I'd heard some song about making new friends for the third time, it was time to act. The girls didn't appear to need entertainment, but I had planned something fun for just this opportunity and didn't want to lose my chance at adding value to today's festivities. I checked around us. None of the moms were nearby as they handled some mysterious camping setup process by the tents.

"Hey, girls. Want to see something cool?"

Skye and a few of the others turned to watch me carry the supplies I'd brought into the middle of the firepit.

"Have you ever seen nucleation in action?" I asked.

A few stepped back in alarm, perhaps thinking I'd said nuclear reaction. With their now undivided attention, I asked for volunteers. Pointing at Skye and a girl next to her who shared the same curly red hair of her not-so-welcoming mother, I whispered some instructions and handed over the supplies.

When all was ready, I started the countdown from ten.

The girls joined in, and we were yelling by the time we reached "Three … Two … One …"

I had told Skye and her fellow volunteer to run after they dropped their Mentos candies into the soda bottles. However, I forgot to warn the watchers to step back. Skye's bottle gushed up almost ten feet before splattering the girls who stood in the front row. And perhaps I also hadn't emphasized the importance of making sure the bottles were stable on the ground. The other girl's bottle of orange soda tipped over, spraying her and a swath of girls in its path.

The screams and giggles brought me unwanted attention, and the other adults hurried over from the tents. Mrs. Payne blew her whistle like she was trying to stop a world war. Eventually, everyone quieted down. Either that or I temporarily lost my hearing.

Mrs. Payne squinted at me, both hands on her hips. "Laney

told me you were an engineer, so you can't be a complete idiot." Delivered in her outdoor voice, the biting words stung. "You really had to work hard to do something this dumb." She shook her head and let out an exasperated sigh. "Now the girls will be sticky until tomorrow, and we have to move to the other firepit."

Mrs. Payne took a deep breath while continuing to glare at me. She then looked from side to side around the campsite, searching for something to keep me out of her hair—also known as my next opportunity to fail.

Finally, she narrowed her eyes and said, "I need you to find some 'special' Girl Scout fire rocks for the fire pit. They grow in a unique place, a long way down the trail. That trail." She pointed to the woods in the opposite direction of the campsite.

The existing, well-formed circle of stones ringing each fire pit made it abundantly clear that she'd handed me a sham project. I wasn't going to put up with her attempt to sideline me. I'd had enough of past managers who assigned silly, make-work tasks out of laziness or stupidity. In fact, I'd quit my last company after one too many "bring me a rock" exercises that made me so aggravated I would stew in frustration for days. This attempt to get me out of the way wasn't going to slip past me.

I rubbed my head as I considered my response. Out of my element, I needed a moment to ponder how to best tell off someone who could drown out my words with one blow of her whistle. Over Mrs. Payne's shoulder, Skye watched me, soda dripping off her hair and nose. Shifting my glance from Skye's pleading look back to Mrs. Payne's stern face, I swallowed as my pride sank like a rock to the pit of my stomach. "Okay."

Heigh-ho, heigh-ho. Off into the forest I headed, whistling under my breath. At least I couldn't fail at a meaningless task of finding make-believe fire rocks.

A cool breeze blew through the woods up from the ocean

located only a few miles from the Santa Cruz Mountains, providing the perfect balance as the day started to warm up and the morning fog burned off. This close to the ocean, it only grew sunny late in the morning. Hanging out in the forest by myself turned out not to be so bad, as long as there was no Payne involved.

The path alternated between dark, shady areas of tree trunks and sun-speckled bushes wherever beams of light broke through the gaps in the branches and leaves high above me. I kept half an eye open for any special rocks so I could bring something back to the campsite.

After about fifteen minutes, I'd wandered far enough into the woods that the noise from the campsite had faded. I thought this might be a good moment to find a B.I.F.F.Y. spot all to myself, so I stepped off the trail by a clump of thick Sequoia trees. A small clearing appeared behind the trees, with a sunbeam illuminating the ground as if a light had been left on for me. I glanced back to ensure my privacy and saw that no one had followed me.

Turning back to attend to my business, I looked to the other side of the clearing and froze.

Someone lay on the ground. Dead.

2

Saturday Morning

Well, maybe dead. It didn't look good, but I couldn't tell from across the clearing. I took a deep breath to steel myself and stepped closer to check.

The person seemed to be a man. Although his shoulders and head were obscured by shadows, the beam of sunlight illuminated his chest and legs. He wore jeans and a T-shirt.

I edged closer. Maybe he was taking a nap. Although I would never sleep on the forest floor amidst all the leaves, bugs, and who knows what else, some people were strange that way. However, the man didn't move when I nudged him with my foot.

Perhaps he'd had a heart attack and needed CPR. I bent over and touched his arm.

It was cool, clammy, and a bit stiff.

I threw up.

I couldn't help it, although I managed to avoid throwing up on the body. People weren't supposed to feel like that. Stumbling back a few steps, I shouted, "Hey!"

My shout came out more like a hoarse whisper, which wouldn't have notified someone a dozen steps away, let alone the others at the campsite.

Shaking my thoughts out of their bewildered tangle, I went to get help. Half staggering in shock, I shuffled as fast as I could along the path back to the campground.

My voice had recovered by the time I emerged from the forest, disheveled, sweaty, and covered with leaves. I shouted again, causing some of the women to glance at me from across the clearing, grimacing in disgust at my disreputable condition as they tried to figure out what I'd done this time. Cupping my hands to my mouth, I tried a third time, shouting in an even louder voice, "Help!"

That was the magic word. A few women started toward me while one of the girls grabbed Mrs. Payne and pointed to me. She blew her whistle three times and the whole troop rushed over, stopping a few steps away from me as they noticed my condition.

"It's a dead guy. He's down there. And dead." I panted as I pointed back down the trail.

As the girls and moms took an extra step back from me, Mrs. Payne swung into action, throwing out instructions almost faster than I could follow. She directed one mom to call 9-1-1, sent several others to the park entrance to flag down the ambulance, assigned most of the moms to corral the girls by the picnic tables, asked two other moms to come with her, and then turned back to me. Flipping open a flap on her vest, she pulled out her emergency first-aid kit. "Show us where he is."

Still stunned by my discovery and her rapid response, I opened my mouth but no words came out.

She clapped me on the back so hard I stumbled forward. "Come on, man, there's no time to waste."

Not wanting to argue that her first-aid kit wouldn't be much use, I headed back down the trail to the body with my new entourage in tow.

When we reached the clearing, Mrs. Payne knelt down with her first-aid kit and touched his arm.

Despite her best efforts, the dead guy stayed dead. She didn't throw up, either. Girl Scout troop leaders were tough.

On our trek back to the landing I had caught my breath and found my wits, so I tried to figure out what to do next. For better or worse, I'd watched enough detective shows during my lifetime to know what *not* to do. I made sure not to touch the body or contaminate the scene, at least not any more than I already had.

Then I pulled out my phone.

Mrs. Payne scoffed. "We already called 9-1-1, and there's no signal this far from the campground anyway."

"I know." I didn't want to explain that I had purchased a specialized medical app last month and wanted to test it out. I bought it after Laney had almost been killed so I'd be prepared in case something else happened. It didn't hurt that the app was created by a startup that also appreciated *Star Trek*, calling their app Tricorder.

Trying to avoid looking at the body, I opened the app. With my stomach still unsettled, I preferred to focus on my new toy, or even on how phones had evolved since the first smartphones came to market back in my youth. I chose the comprehensive imaging option and aimed the phone's camera at the guy's feet.

"You're taking pictures?" One of the moms flinched away from me in disgust.

"It's a medical app." I quickly turned off the phone's volume—this wasn't the time to showcase the app's really cool sound effects. It took infrared, ultraviolet, slow motion, and high-resolution images, as well as executed some other fancy-sounding medical analyses to provide the user with an unofficial diagnosis.

My hands trembled a bit as I rotated the phone slowly up the body, wondering what the app would do when confronted with an actual dead person. Last week, Megan had been most disappointed after attempting to claim a mysterious illness had struck her and the app had reported her as healthy. Laney had teased me that only a geek would need an app to tell him that a child was lying to get out of a school project.

I let my eyes dwell on the guy's badly sunburnt hands and arms before reluctantly lifting the phone to catch his face.

My heart almost stopped.

I knew him.

This time, I threw up on the body.

The dead guy was Larry, my old friend and part of my monthly poker group.

I toppled away, almost falling to the ground before Mrs. Payne and one of the other moms caught me. They guided me out of the landing and sat me down on the hiking trail. Despite the leaves and bugs, I didn't resist.

What was Larry doing lying dead in the middle of the forest?

How had he died?

Larry was a scientist, a biologist who spent his days behind a lab bench. Only last month he mentioned he'd been promoted to run a new research project. He worked at Sirius Innovation in their biotech division, their largest team. Sirius had made an offer to acquire Rover, and once the acquisition was finalized, I expected to see Larry more often, though certainly not today—and dead.

When I felt a bit better, I stood up to get away from all the bugs and dirt. As the women escorted me back to the campsite, my mind was in a daze. Friends of mine didn't go hiking and then wind up dead in the middle of a forest. Going forward, that would have to be my new requirement for all friends. I'd let them know as soon as I got back to civilization.

When the Santa Cruz County Sheriff's deputies arrived, I was sitting on a rock by myself at the side of the campsite. The two deputies glanced at me before Mrs. Payne took charge and brought them down the trail without me.

For some time, I stayed where I was, staring at the ground but not seeing anything.

"Excuse me. I understand you discovered the body?" A female deputy stood in front of me.

"Larry." My friend had a name.

The deputy squinted at me. "Larry, do you have a last name and some ID?"

Now she was just being dumb. "I'm not Larry. He's Larry. Or he was." My voice caught in my throat.

"You knew him?" Her eyebrows rose in surprise.

This was getting annoying. "Well, of course. I've known him since college. He's in my poker group, although he isn't any good. He still owes me from last time." I couldn't believe I wouldn't see him again. I reached into my jacket for a bandana, which had been on the required packing list, to wipe away the tears that threatened to spill out of my eyes.

"Sir! Remove your hands from your pockets slowly and stand up." She had backed up a step and was pointing her gun at me.

I jumped to my feet with my hands in the air. "Whoa! What's going on? Why are you pointing your gun at me?"

"Sir, calm down. And don't move." She gestured to her partner, a stocky Asian officer, who hurried over to us.

He approached me from the side, careful not to get between her gun and me. Then he grabbed my arms, holding them in one strong hand behind me while patting me down.

"What are you doing? I didn't do anything." Adrenalin raced through my body.

He pulled my wallet out of my back pocket and held it behind me.

"Hey, that's mine. You can't take my wallet." My voice rose as all my pent-up emotions flowed out.

"Marty Golden," he announced to his partner after checking out my driver's license.

"What's Larry's last name?" she asked me.

"Cohen. Can't you check his license without attacking me?" I tugged my hands, trying to free myself from the deputy's grasp.

"He didn't have any ID on him," he said, releasing me.

"So how much money did he owe you? And where were you earlier this morning?" the female deputy asked as she lowered her gun.

I bristled at the implied accusation. "Maybe twenty dollars, if that. I've been here with the Girl Scouts all morning until I found him."

"You're a Girl Scout, huh?" She still sounded skeptical. "Is your friend a Girl Scout too? What was he doing here?"

If she was trying to provoke me, it was working. "I don't know. Isn't that what you're supposed to figure out?"

"You're a wise guy, is that it? You think this is funny? What part of the Girl Scout activities included walking by yourself a half mile away on a trail that led straight to your friend?"

I blushed. "I ... I was not the best with the campsite chores so the troop leader sent me to do something else on my own. Ask her."

"Oh, we will." The female deputy put her gun away, but not her attitude. "If he's such a good friend, why'd you nail him with your vomit? Twice. Is that how you treat your friends?"

I snapped, "It was only once. It sure wasn't part of my day's plan to throw up all over a dead friend lying in the middle of a forest and then get accosted by some two-bit county deputies."

The male deputy grabbed my shirt and pulled me close enough that I could smell the coffee on his breath. "Watch your step, buddy." He stared at me with cold, dark eyes for a moment before pushing me away. "Crawl back under your rock and don't bother anyone." He tossed my wallet to the ground.

My brain caught up before my mouth sounded off again, so I

decided not to point out that if I hadn't been watching my step, I wouldn't have found Larry at all.

The deputies put their heads together before the woman took out a notebook and wrote something in it.

I hoped today wouldn't end with me visiting the Santa Cruz County Sheriff's office.

Turning their backs on me, the deputies walked off together toward the girls and moms, who were still gaping at us from the picnic tables.

This left me alone to wonder what had happened to Larry's wallet. And Larry.

Much of the next few hours flew by in a blur. I stayed on my rock, looking away from the trail and watching the trees sway in the breeze. Larry and I had first met during freshman year in college when we lived next door to each other in the same dorm. We became friends and had stayed in contact over all these years. Although he'd moved around a bit, he had lived in Silicon Valley for at least a decade.

As the sheriffs led the paramedics down the trail to the body, the moms resumed their camping preparations. The girls flitted around, helping and gossiping.

Seeing the coast had cleared, Skye wandered over with some of her friends, who were whispering to each other and pretending to ignore my presence. Surprised that Skye was still willing to talk to someone deemed a Girl Scout pariah, I looked up at her without speaking.

"Are you okay, Uncle Marty?" she asked as her friends quieted behind her.

"Maybe not the best. Larry is—or, I guess, was—a good friend of mine." My voice caught in my throat.

Skye surprised me again by leaning in and giving me a quick hug.

As I hugged her back, I glanced up at the other girls. They

were edging away from us, looking uncomfortable, no longer sure if they wanted to hang around this unseemly display of familial affection toward an unstable uncle. Too many unpredictable things had happened around me even for Girl Scouts who were taught to "be prepared." Or maybe that was the Boy Scouts?

I couldn't even remember the right motto.

A few of the girls started to shift their feet, preparing to ditch their friend and see if something more interesting was happening near the swarm of police, paramedics, and medical examiners.

I continued, "I think I upset the deputies. I was going to show them pictures of Larry from a special app on my phone, but I don't think they want to talk to me now."

Over Skye's shoulder, several of the girls glanced at each other, suddenly looking more alert. The curly-haired redhead who had gotten sprayed with orange soda raised her eyebrows and asked, "Can we see the pictures?"

The whole clump of girls swayed forward, apprehensive yet eager to see pictures of a dead person since their mothers had banned them from approaching Larry's body.

Maybe it wasn't my smartest move, but these girls had all seen plenty of dead bodies on TV and in the movies, and those were often far more gruesome than Larry, with blood, gore, and missing body parts. Larry just looked asleep under the trees. Besides, I hadn't had a chance to look at the pictures either. The app's sample images had resembled forensics from one of those criminal investigation shows.

Figuring there wouldn't be any harm in it, I took out my phone, flicked on the volume, and held it so we could all see as I opened the app again.

The girls stepped forward in anticipation, forming a tight knot around Skye and me.

My phone buzzed and a voice said, "Seek urgent medical attention."

I almost dropped the phone until realizing that the app had completed its analysis and was providing its diagnosis. Guess the engineers had never intended it to assess a dead body. Knowing how these things work in companies, I figured their lawyers instructed the engineers not to give a customer any scary results. That would be bad for customer satisfaction.

Better to leave the bad news to an actual doctor. Or lawyer. But if the app wouldn't tell me that a cold body was dead, would it inform me of other serious conditions it detected? What was the use of having an app that didn't give you accurate and important information?

"Uncle Marty!" Skye interrupted my train of thought.

I'd distracted myself again. This happened on a regular basis. The girls were looking at me with puzzled expressions as they waited impatiently to see something exciting. I flicked the screen to reveal the first image.

An infrared image of Larry appeared. His body, mostly tinted in unnatural-looking shades of green and blue, had blotchy streaks of brighter yellow and red on his arms, starting from the backs of his wrists. On the infrared image, none of Larry's features were distinct. Only his outlined body, colored like a rainbow, showed on the screen.

The redhead said, "Cool," and leaned in even closer.

Another girl, wearing a faded Girl Scout hat over a blonde ponytail, said, "Eww, that's gross, not cool." She left the circle and trotted back to the tents.

"What's that?" asked the redhead, pointing to the blotchy yellow and red area on Larry's arms.

The other girls leaned over to see closer, our heads almost touching as we huddled over the phone.

I zoomed in to see the blotches expand on the unnatural blue body. "That must be his sunburn."

As I spoke, the unlikelihood of the situation struck me. Larry worked in a lab all week. Today was Saturday, and I'd found him no later than ten o'clock this morning. If he'd gone hiking earlier today, he couldn't have gotten sunburnt before dying. The sun had barely burned off the heavy fog when we got to the campground. It was possible he took yesterday off and got sunburnt then, but he'd talked about how busy things were at work since he started on the special project.

Since the Santa Cruz County deputies didn't seem willing to talk to me again, I needed to call Mace and ask him to look into Larry's sunburn and whether he'd taken Friday off work.

Mace Jackson, a sergeant in the San Jose Police Department, served as my imaginary action-hero partner. He looked like an action hero, even if he might not agree to the partner part. Only last month he had helped me save Laney from a homicidal psychopath. Afterwards, he'd gotten some good press, so I was sure he'd be ready to talk to me again.

"What are you doing?" asked an adult voice in a strident tone.

I looked up to see the mom with the puffy jacket and curly red hair standing in front of me, frowning and staring at me intensely. Preoccupied with thoughts of Larry's sunburn and Mace, I hadn't noticed anyone approaching us.

"Showing pictures of Larry from my special app," I answered with enthusiasm as I looked down at my phone again. This app had really cool technology. I couldn't figure out how they processed the different images without my phone needing special lenses. I'd have to do some internet research when I got home.

"You're what?" Her voice grew louder as her eyebrows rose and her expression turned simultaneously astonished and angry.

Hearing her anger, I looked up, my thoughts still stuck on the app. "It's like one of those tricorders," I answered in a weak voice.

I should have kept my mouth shut. There was no way to dig myself out of this grave, so to speak.

"I ..." She tried to speak to me, then gave up and redirected her energy to the clump of girls around me. She grabbed her daughter by the arm and yanked her away from me. "Let's go, girls, you need to come with me." She shooed the girls away, even Skye, who wasn't hers to shoo.

"From *Star Trek*," I mumbled to no one.

As Skye walked away, she looked back at me and gave me a grin and a small wave.

I'd recovered some status with her and her friends by showing them a dead body. Too bad it happened to be Larry.

A minute after the group reached the rest of the troop, Mrs. Payne broke away and strode over to me, whistle bouncing on her chest.

I braced myself for a tongue lashing. Or being forced to do push-ups.

"Mr. Golden, I think it's best if you head home now." From Mrs. Payne's expression, it was clear that puffy-jacket mom had tattled on me.

"But Skye's been looking forward to this campout for weeks." I wasn't thinking straight or I'd have taken the excuse to bail on the Girl Scouts, their B.I.F.F.Y., and the whole camping business. I still liked their cookies, though.

She put her hands on her hips. "She can stay. You need to go."

"What?" I didn't understand. Laney had coerced me into coming as Skye's chaperone, a requirement for her to participate in this long-awaited weekend's activities.

"We'll take care of Skye and bring her back tomorrow. You go. Now."

I might not pick up on social cues at all the appropriate times, but even an idiot could tell she didn't want me here.

Without answering aloud, I nodded. In silence, we walked back to the tables where I said goodbye to Skye, picked up my things, and left the campground.

In the parking lot, my Rover app told me a car wouldn't arrive to take me home for at least thirty minutes. Even with Rover's expanding market, it didn't make sense to keep a shared car idling in the middle of the Santa Cruz Mountains on the off chance that a client standing in an isolated campground needed a ride.

No longer feeling like interacting with anyone, I stayed out in the parking lot, standing on the far side of the ambulance, out of sight. Even before I discovered Larry, today had been headed into the toilet, or, rather, the B.I.F.F.Y.—which was even worse.

I decided to call Mace while I waited, but he didn't answer, probably because he was busy with another case. I had just started to leave him a message when the paramedics surprised me by pushing a gurney around the back of the ambulance. I dropped my phone in the middle of my message, then accidentally disconnected the call when I picked it back up.

The EMTs, both trim and sporting crewcuts, laughed at my clumsiness as they opened the back of the ambulance and loaded Larry's body. One of them said, "Boy, you really pissed off Chung."

"Who?" I pissed off lots of people so it was helpful to keep them straight.

"The deputy you spoke to," he said, as if that would narrow things down for me. "If I were you, I'd leave now so he doesn't give you a ticket or arrest you for something. He and his partner are not pleased with you."

I sighed. "I'm waiting for my ride, but it will be at least thirty minutes."

"Well, I suppose we could give you a ride." He looked at his partner, who shrugged.

"Thanks. That would be great." The sooner I got out of here, the better. I canceled my Rover car.

"Don't say thanks yet," said the other EMT as he took a step back from me. "You smell like vomit, so you're riding in the back with him." He jabbed a finger at Larry's shrouded body. "And you haven't seen how my partner drives." Shaking his head, he laughed at his own joke as he helped his partner load the gurney into the back before climbing into the passenger seat.

I rode in the back, alone with my thoughts and Larry, while clinging to the seat during the roller coaster ride along Highway 17 and breathing through my mouth.

3

Sunday Morning

The phone woke me earlier on Sunday than I'd planned to get up. "Hello," I mumbled.

"Hi, Marty, this is Lauren. Isn't this the most terrible news? I'm all broken up. Did you ... did you really find him?" The voice was loud and way too energetic for a Sunday morning.

"Who is this?" I mumbled again as I sat up and wiped my face with my other hand.

"Marty! It's me. Lauren, Lauren Cohen."

"Lori?"

"I go by Lauren now. It sounds much more elegant than Lori. Don't you think?" Lauren actually waited for a response.

"Oh. Sure." She called to ask me about her name change? Focusing instead on her brother, I said, "I'm sorry for your loss." It was formulaic, but I didn't know what else to say. I hadn't seen Lori ... Lauren ... since graduating from college. Two years younger than Larry and me, she'd been excited to go out with me, a junior, when she first got to college. After a couple of dates, the excitement wore off and she dumped me when she decided she could do better. "How'd you get my number?"

"The police gave it to me. They called me last night to tell me about Larry. I asked them if they knew of any of Larry's friends in town and they told me you had found him."

"Yeah." I had not slept well last night, waking up several times with thoughts of Larry and feeling phantom leaves and bugs crawling over me in my dreams.

"So, can you do it?"

My mind must have wandered. "What? Sorry. Do what?"

"Still going off in your own world, huh? Well, anyway, I asked if you could stop by his house today and help his neighbor set it up for a shiva memorial service."

Shiva was sort of a Jewish memorial condolence call after the funeral to Larry's family and the bereaved mourners. Typically, there would be a short prayer service for the deceased, followed by food—a requirement for all Jewish events. It might have been one of the Ten Commandments. Sometimes you needed food to plan upcoming Jewish events that involved more food. Then, everyone talked about what they would eat at their next meal. This was especially true during a Jewish family get-together for a wedding, bar mitzvah, shiva, Mahjong game, or any other random family event.

I scratched my head in confusion. "I thought the police said they'd be doing an autopsy before releasing his body. Did they finish it so fast? And isn't there supposed to be a funeral before the shiva?" Although I was no religious expert, some things were pretty straightforward, even to me.

"You know, that rabbi up there in San Jose was very accommodating. He said we could hold a shiva-like ceremony on Monday since we don't know when they'll release his body. The rabbi said it's good to get the grieving process started right away."

Lauren's peppy voice sounded as if she was anything but grieving. I was starting to get a headache, so I rubbed my temples and tried to concentrate.

She continued, "And we're leaving for vacation on Tuesday, so I need to get this taken care of before our flight."

I sighed. "Okay, I'll go over there this morning."

"Hawaii. We've got this amazing condo for the week, right on the beach." As my actual response registered, Lauren added, "Great. Thanks, Marty. I'll see you tomorrow night. It'll be great to catch up after all these years. I've gotta go now, though. I've got a million errands to take care of before our vacation." She sighed. "And now I have to take this trip to San Jose." She hung up before I could say goodbye.

After I showered and ate, I took a Rover to Larry's house. Getting out of the car, I was disconcerted to see Larry's car parked in his driveway like nothing was wrong. I stood there looking at it, half expecting Larry to step out of the driver's side to greet me. Gazing at his car sparked some questions. How had Larry gotten to the Santa Cruz park without it? Had he gone with someone? Why hadn't they called 9-1-1 to save him?

The neighbor's screen door banged open, startling me out of my introspection. I looked up to see an old woman standing in the doorway with both arms perched on her hips. I've learned not to ask a woman her age, but some of her wrinkles had wrinkles.

"Stop standing there looking at the car and come help. I'm too old to do everything by myself, you know." She spoke in a pleasant, if direct, voice.

I walked the few steps to her porch, then stopped in confusion as she stepped outside and pulled the screen door closed behind herself.

"Well now, sonny, I don't got me all day. We've got to get ready for this here shiva thing for tomorrow for dear departed Larry."

"I'm sorry …"

The woman gave a friendly laugh and patted my shoulder. "Oh, that's all right. You can call me Carmela. I've lived in this house for over forty years now. I sit in the front yard most of the day and talk like this to everyone and everything that walks by my house. Keeps me from getting lonely. I don't care if it's a girl, boy, woman, dog, cat, squirrel or even a man. I say hello to all of them and give them a little poke to make sure they're paying attention. Wakes them right up now, it does." She burst out laughing.

Although still confused, I noticed where men fell in her hierarchy. "I'm Marty. I'm here to—"

Carmela interrupted, "Of course you are. Of course. Come on, you can help me get some extra chairs from Larry's house." With a slight limp, she eased down the porch steps and headed next door.

"Why are we getting the chairs? Aren't we holding the service at Larry's house?" Despite Carmela's slow pace, I still felt left behind in this conversation.

"You haven't been to his house, now have you?"

At my head shake, Carmela cackled. "You'll see, you'll see, soon enough." She laughed again, enjoying her surprise in advance.

I followed her slow, halting steps to Larry's house. Instead of continuing to the front door, Carmela turned down the path alongside the house, heading to the backyard.

"Wouldn't the front door be easier?" I asked.

Carmela only responded with another chuckle before repeating, "You'll see, you'll see."

Carmela had an odd sense of humor. Yet, if I had to grow old, I wanted to be as happy as she was. Amusing myself wouldn't be anything new to me. I hoped I would reach her age. After all, the alternative was far less appealing.

When we reached the back door after passing Larry's pool, Carmela paused and glanced at me. "Ready?" she asked with a twinkle in her eye, stepping aside to let me enter first.

I pushed the door open and stepped inside his kitchen. My mouth fell open as I stopped dead in my tracks. Stacks of stuff were balanced everywhere. The table, counter, and chairs were overflowing with stuff. Junk, actually. Paper goods and cardboard boxes from Costco, some still full of unopened cartons of food, took up almost the entire kitchen.

Larry had been a hoarder. I never knew.

Sure, his college dorm room had been cluttered, but so was mine. I couldn't remember ever visiting his place in recent years, although that wasn't unusual. We typically met for a meal or at a sports bar to watch a game. His hoarding did explain why he'd always refused to host our poker nights at his place, though. Each time, he had a different excuse—remodel, furniture getting donated, cleaners hadn't come, and so on. He'd been so consistent in his refusals that it had become something of a standing joke, and we eventually stopped asking. After seeing this, I felt bad for making fun of him. Was it possible to feel retroactive embarrassment?

I didn't notice any open food around, so Larry wasn't a slob, just a hoarder. Cases of Red Bull were stacked everywhere. I had thought only engineers got hooked on Red Bull, not biologists. Chugging Red Bull was almost a rite of passage during late-night college coding sessions. Our professors had told us that before Red Bull came out, they'd gotten hooked on Mountain Dew when they were young. That just seemed gross.

Maybe Red Bull also powered crazy nights grinding away in the lab doing gene editing as biologists like Larry came up with wilder and wilder ideas for new creatures. Scary thought.

After edging out of the kitchen, a musty, dusty odor hit me and I stifled a sneeze. Larry had converted his home into a storehouse of bookshelves, stacks of boxes, and folders full of paper. He'd created aisles out of all the stacks, some leading off a main route in neat rows, others winding around the room's nooks and crannies. A few paths meandered around outsized pieces of broken electronic equipment in various stages of disrepair. Some of the stacks of boxes, books, and papers rose well over my head, almost touching the eight-foot ceiling.

Baited rat traps guarded the aisles. Fortunately, they all looked empty to me. My parents' etiquette lessons were effective enough to get me to help out for a close friend's shiva and carry some chairs, but I drew the line at cleaning out rotting rat traps.

In his organizational obsessiveness, Larry had stuck neat hand-printed signs on different stacks, almost like his own version of grocery store aisles. No numbers yet, so he hadn't quite reached the point of inventing a new Dewey Decimal System. I browsed the aisles, more in amazement than anything else.

I paused at the stack labeled "San Francisco Giants," because, well, Giants. Larry had clipped newspaper articles about Giants' players going back for years. Careful to avoid toppling the stack, I pulled out a folder from a carton at random and got absorbed reading about a long-ago favorite player.

Carmela startled me by clearing her throat. I looked up from my reading to see her standing in the aisle not far from me. "This is something, isn't it? I've only been in here a few times myself. I can't rightly say how he and that dog both fit in here."

All I could do was nod. Although I'd heard of hoarding, I'd never known anyone who did it. Well, at least I hadn't realized I'd known a hoarder.

Carmela shuffled a few feet farther and pointed a gnarled finger over the top of a shorter stack. "You can see why we came in the back." She laughed again, pleased with herself.

I looked in the direction she pointed. Piles of unsorted clothes, books, mail, and other objects surrounded the front door. They almost enclosed the doorway, as if Larry had created stacks all the way out his front door, leaving no clear path to the rest of the house. Another maze of stacks, high enough to block the view of the upstairs landing from below, disappeared up the stairs.

Carmela followed my glance. "Yeah, it continues upstairs, but not as bad."

A sign for Sirius Innovation was taped onto a large stack a row over from where I stood. Navigating to it, I found that Larry had folders labeled by month and year piling up nearly to the ceiling. He'd started a second stack for Sirius, this one only chest-high, that had more recent paperwork. Curious, I pulled the folder off the top and fanned through it. He had printouts of company memos, scientific reports, emails, and all sorts of random documents. I could understand keeping a copy of something important that you worked on, but why keep random presentations or documents that weren't even yours? An obsessive collection of worthless paperwork. I yawned just thinking about it.

Perhaps this explained what happened to all those random faxes and printouts that always seemed to accumulate by the company printer. Although I tried to grab my printouts immediately, sometimes I got distracted. If I made it to the printer much later, they were always missing. They never seemed to be in the nearby recycling or trash bins, especially if there was an urgent need for that printout. At Sirius, Larry must have served as the collector of last resort.

Pondering who served this role at Rover led me to wonder if Larry had any materials about my company now that Sirius had decided to buy us. I started flipping through the pages in the top folder, looking for any mentions of Rover.

"Hey, I know this guy." The name of my colleague, Raj, was listed on a weekly calendar printout for a meeting tomorrow with Doug Samerson, CEO of Sirius Innovation.

Raj, a recent immigrant from India, was my closest friend at work. I enjoyed his company, and he seemed to like mine. We sat next to each other at work and often ate our lunches at our desks together. Raj was super smart, spoke multiple languages, and had a few degrees. A brilliant engineer, he also had a good sense of humor. Just like me.

I didn't understand why he would be meeting with Doug Samerson, who was building a reputation as an eccentric, and somewhat successful, serial entrepreneur. He hadn't yet achieved the status of Steve Jobs of Apple, or Elon Musk of Tesla, but not for lack of trying. Whenever I checked out his keynote speeches online, he came across as a bit wacky. Not surprising, as most executives had a screw loose somewhere. The ones aspiring to be visionary leaders often had a carton of screws rolling around inside their heads.

So why was Raj meeting with Samerson? And why hadn't he said something to me about it?

Carmela was tired of standing around. "Now sonny, don't you be going all crazy in the head like ole Larry. Let's leave all his junk alone and git on out of here before my heart gives out from all this standing."

I set the folder on the stack. There was no point making her suffer. Neither Raj's name nor mine appeared on the next pages—various legal forms and scientific reports—so I followed her out of Larry's overstuffed house. At Carmela's request, I picked up four folding chairs from Larry's kitchen to take back to her house.

Locking the back door behind us, Carmela bent down and placed a key in a fake rock at the side of the back porch. As she creaked back up, she waggled a finger at me. "Now don't you be telling all the criminals how to break into Larry's house. That wouldn't be neighborly of you."

If she'd ever met my mother, she would have known she didn't need to tell me not to steal, even though, technically, I wasn't Larry's neighbor.

Sneaking into his house brought another question to mind. "Have the police been here yet?"

"I surely haven't seen any stop by, and I would know. They

called me yesterday around supper from way down in Santa Cruz and asked about anyone living with Larry. I told them it was just Larry and his dog."

Deciding it was best not to share my as-yet-unproven theories about Larry's untimely demise, I only responded, "Just wondered."

Carmela and I continued to chat about Larry as we ambled around the side of his house and into his small front yard while I lugged the four folding chairs.

A woman in her thirties wearing workout gear that highlighted her muscular, toned build burst out of the house on the other side of Larry's and hustled to her car.

Carmela called out to her, "Gloria, you're always on the run now."

"I have to get to a class." Gloria didn't even look up.

"Will you be able to make it for Larry's shiva service tomorrow? I'm sure it will be lovely."

"I don't want to talk about him." As Gloria dismissed Larry with a wave toward his house, her keys flew out of her hand. She frowned and stomped around her car to retrieve them. When she noticed me standing next to Carmela, she asked, "Is this guy taking his damn dog?"

Carmela gave a belly laugh. "Goodness no, he's helping me get ready for the shiva. I told the police that I'd take care of the dog for a few days so they could contact Larry's family." She snorted to herself. "I surely know you don't want him. Not after—"

Gloria jerked up out of her crouch. "Stop! We agreed not to talk about the poisoning." As she realized her slip in front of me, she cursed.

Startled, I looked more closely at her. "You poisoned his dog? Or Larry?" I didn't remember Larry mentioning anything about poisoning. Had Gloria tried to kill Larry, or his dog, before? Had she been more successful yesterday in killing Larry?

"Like it mattered if one got poisoned before the other. That dog licked his plates. And Larry always let it lick him on the face. It was disgusting."

Although she hadn't answered my question, I had to agree with her. All sorts of disgusting things went into dogs' mouths. They'd lick or sniff everything—the stinkier, the better. People who let their dogs lick their plates, or their faces, were just asking to get sick.

Then, something she had said struck me. "How did you know the dog licked his plates?"

Gloria's face reddened as she fumbled with her keys, trying to unlock her car door.

Carmela said, "Never mind all that. What's done is done. No sense digging up buried secrets." Then she blushed at the incongruity of her words right before Larry's memorial service.

I was still bothered by the idea that Gloria might have wanted to kill Larry, at least once before. "When did you do this? And where were you yesterday?" Had Gloria poisoned Larry again and dumped his body in the woods? She looked fit enough to carry him.

Gloria blew a raspberry at me. "Ask that damn dog of his. Yesterday, it barked at me all day long. Always running in circles around his pool, barking at everything. No room for a dog in that house anyway." She blushed again, then continued before I could interrupt. "Barking at all times of the day and night. Enough to drive a person crazy. He never did anything about it." She looked at Carmela. "How come it never drove you crazy?"

Carmela reached up to her right ear and pulled out a tiny hearing aid. "When I want some peace and quiet, I turn off my hearing aids. Blessed silence. Praise be." She made a gesture to the heavens and then pushed the hearing aid back into her ear. Tugging at my arm, she said, "Come on, sonny, help me back home. I've got to sit down again before my heart plumb gives out."

I still wanted to ask how Gloria knew so much about what

happened on the other side of a six-foot fence. Had something gone on between her and Larry? Or had she finally decided to pay Larry back for not quieting his dog?

Before I could finish formulating my question, Gloria scrambled into her car and roared off. I'd have to follow up another time.

As I escorted Carmela on her slow journey back to her house, I asked, "Is Gloria a student somewhere?"

Carmela thought this was funny. "Oh silly, she was talking about some exercise class. Crosstown? Maybe it was crosswords?" She laughed at her own poor memory.

"CrossFit?"

Carmela nodded. "Yeah, that sounds right. She got into that big time a few years ago and lost a lot of weight. Right after she and Larry ... Well, never mind all that. Did you know she works at Sirius too?" Carmela snorted and shook her head as she muttered something quietly to herself.

My folks would have been proud of my manners. I made sure Carmela got safely inside before taking out my phone. I needed to leave another voicemail for Mace and then call Raj. I signaled for a Rover car to pick me up while I composed my thoughts.

Gloria and Larry both worked at Sirius, the same company that was buying Rover and would soon be paying my salary. She and Larry had an unexplained past that involved poison. And she kept secrets. Sometimes, people were killed because of secrets.

And why did Raj have a meeting with the CEO of Sirius tomorrow that he hadn't told me about? Friends didn't keep secrets like that from each other.

As my Rover car pulled away from the curb, I sat back, still staring at my phone, pondering whether to tell Mace that Gloria might have killed Larry out of rage over his dog or if something else had happened between them. Before calling Mace this time, I would try my hardest to do a good job on the message.

Gloria, I think I've got your number.

4

Sunday Afternoon

My mother never taught me the proper etiquette for whether you should go out with a new girlfriend during the same weekend you discover a friend's body in the woods. As I've gotten older, I've discovered a disturbing number of lessons my parents left out of my upbringing.

Meghan, who was new enough as my girlfriend that I wasn't even quite sure if I should describe her like that, had insisted we keep our plans to take Laney and Skye out for dinner on Sunday, especially now that Laney had broken her ankle. I'd been married before, and dated other women, so I knew that settled things. Besides, it felt good that she was trying to make me feel a little better about Larry's death by distracting me.

I couldn't even talk to the rest of the poker group about Larry. When the EMTs had dropped me off, they relayed instructions from the deputies insisting that I wait until Monday morning before telling anyone else what happened. Something about needing to wait until news of his death was officially released and ongoing delays with autopsies at the county coroner's office.

As if an entire troop of Girl Scouts and their mothers wouldn't be telling everyone what happened. Not to mention Carmela and Gloria. I didn't want to, yet I followed their rules, although I still decided to exercise some minor civil disobedience by telling Meghan and Laney. After all, I was still pissed at the deputies for how they treated me.

Although going out might not have been proper etiquette to Ms. Manners, it cleared the bar for Meghan. Not that a quick stroll through the mall with my girlfriend followed by a burger with my sister and niece made for an especially romantic or elegant date.

Meghan and I had met only last month when she became a suspect in my sister's attempted murder. Our relationship had a rough start that got worse when my niece, Megan, discovered that Meghan shared her name, but chocolate chip pancakes quickly resolved that situation. Meghan was an environmental scientist with a PhD. She was smart, ingenious, and had an obvious sense of humor since she seemed to like me. I liked her too. We made a good team. That was as deep as I usually got.

Meghan suggested we go to the mall so I could pick up a get-well gift for Laney. My objection that I'd already given her the gift of going to the Girl Scout campout in the wilderness in her place earned me a brief, withering look. Meghan observed that I had lasted only four hours in the wilderness and hadn't even slept in a sleeping bag. By putting air quotes around "wilderness," she gave the distinct impression that she didn't find my fears of wild animal attacks in the Santa Cruz Girl Scout campground credible. Deciding not to push the issue, I didn't bring up the horrors of the B.I.F.F.Y., seeing as I had never used it. Meghan squeezed my hand anyway as she noticed me avoiding any mention of Larry again.

We walked past one of those mall tea stores. Not a tea shop that served tea in a cup that normal people drank, but a tea enthusiast's store with tea cups, barrels, tea kettles, and other unusual supplies. I merely drank tea. Maybe I wasn't enthusiastic enough.

"Let's see if there's a nice tea for Laney. I'm sure she'd like something calming." Without waiting for a reply, Meghan turned into the store.

I followed her around the store for a few minutes while she picked up what seemed like each individual tea cup in the whole place. Shopping bored me, and this store was the definition of boredom. I was more of a "go straight to the item, buy it, and leave as fast as possible" kind of guy. In other words, a guy.

Leaving Meghan to her own devices, I wandered over to the other side of the store, where clerks holding plates and decorative paper fans stood near barrels. I was hungry. Perhaps they had snacks.

I walked up to a clerk wearing a black apron imprinted with the store's logo and reached out to select a snack from the plate. My hand stopped in mid-air when I saw that the plate contained a small pile of green leaves, twigs, and dirt. She must have just swept up. Definitely not crackers.

Still holding the plate in front of her, the clerk greeted me with a pleasant smile. "Hello, sir. What kind of tea do you like?"

"Green." I pointed to the plate of debris. "What are you doing with that?"

"It's Peppermint Ginger Ginseng tea leaves. You buy them by the ounce and then put them in an infuser."

I had no idea what an infuser was. Wrinkling my nose at the plate's odor, I gave her a polite smile and turned to the next clerk to look for crackers or cheese, or even both if I got lucky.

The second clerk was holding a plate too. Now much more sophisticated in my tea appreciation, I asked, "Is that Peppermint Ginger Ginseng tea also?"

She answered, "It's Monkey-Picked Oolong tea."

I distrusted the sanitary nature of allowing monkeys to pick tea. Sometimes even the human baristas didn't measure up to my sanitary expectations.

"Would you like a sniff?" she asked, and, without waiting, waved her fan to waft the odor of the tea leaves in my direction.

A strong, woodsy smell mixed with jasmine enveloped me.

I sneezed.

"Oh my!" The clerk jerked back, spilling some of the tea on the floor.

The other clerk gasped and stepped over to us. "You sneezed? On the tea?" She wrinkled her nose and grabbed a broom and dustpan.

"It wasn't my fault," I started to justify myself, then blushed as the other customers looked at us. After all, she'd wafted without warning.

My explanation that sneezing was an involuntary bodily function usually caused by foreign particles irritating your nasal mucus didn't help matters. The snickering around us didn't help matters.

The clerks had heard enough. They wafted me out the door. Despite my protests, I didn't much mind, as I'd been in the store too long anyway.

A few minutes later, Meghan found me waiting for her outside the store. "Where'd you go?" She tilted her head to the side as she handed me a package.

"It seemed better for me to wait outside." Changing the subject, I asked, "Did you know they're charging a hundred bucks for a small container of tea?"

"Yes. What's your point?" Meghan shrugged and widened her hazel eyes.

Before I could comment on how pretty her eyes looked today, my mouth ran ahead of my brain and I blurted out, "Well, that's ridiculous. You can get a box of tea bags at the grocery store for just a few dollars."

"It's special tea." Meghan spoke like she was addressing a child.

"It wasn't even green tea," I whined.

She rolled her eyes at me, a move patented by Skye. Perhaps Meghan and Skye had been spending too much time together. "How much did you spend on that bottle of wine at dinner last weekend?"

"That was different. This is a silly gift for my clumsy sister."

"Why? Wasn't it special too?" she asked, a dangerous glint in her eyes.

I swooped in and kissed her. It didn't take a brain surgeon to see that trap coming and avoid answering.

The aroma of more tea wafted over me from the store. Turning my head to the side to avoid Meghan, I sneezed again. "I must be allergic to oolongs or monkeys."

"What?" Meghan laughed, holding on to my arm as she tried not to trip over me after my sudden change of direction. She seemed amused at my change of topics.

In a flash, I remembered the last time I'd seen Larry. Last month, he came to our poker night at another guy's house. He'd sneezed again and again until he went into the bathroom for a tissue.

"Larry was allergic to cats."

"Cats? What?" Meghan pulled on my arm to grab my attention.

"Sorry. My sneezing reminded me that Larry was highly allergic to lots of things. At our poker night, he had an allergy attack from the guy's cat."

Meghan shrugged. "Okay. I'm sorry for him, but what does that matter?"

"I don't know. I should tell the police."

"You're going to tell them he was allergic to cats?" When Meghan said the words aloud, they sounded silly.

"Maybe you're right. The cops didn't like me much anyway." I told her about my encounter with the two deputies.

Meghan worked hard to keep her grin from turning into laughter at my expense. "You do seem to have a way with the police, don't you?"

I didn't respond, because something about Larry's allergies was bothering me. I wanted the police to know everything about Larry in case it could help them explain his death. As we walked back to the car, I pulled out my phone, mentally composing what I'd say to Mace.

*****

"He's a big problem." Fortunately, Laney was referring to her new dog, Buddy, rather than me.

Laney, Meghan, Skye, and I had just finished our dinner at some salad place near Laney's house. I was still hoping a burger would appear. At her worst, Laney still ate heathier than me. With her newly-enforced idleness from her broken ankle, she'd decided to ramp up the healthy-eating effort. No one had consulted me. Dinner felt incomplete.

"Come on, you're still training him," said Meghan.

Buddy weighed almost seventy pounds and came up to my waist. I hadn't liked dogs ever since one jumped at a six-year-old version of me and chased me across three lawns back to my house, barking the whole way. That dog probably thought I was an awesome pace car for his Nascar training. He may not have wanted to do anything more than lick my face, but young me feared I was about to become a chew toy. Since that traumatic moment, I kept away from dogs. If I had to own a pet, I preferred a fish tank, like Laney had. Fish didn't lick people on the face, although one did touch me when I was snorkeling. I could do without that.

"You wouldn't say that if you saw what he did last night." Laney pulled out her phone and leaned over to show it to Meghan, who took a look and burst out laughing.

"Right?" Laney asked. "He's always getting into the laundry and chewing our clothes. Since I haven't been able to get around as well, I didn't get all the clothes put away last night."

Meghan struggled to catch her breath, then took the phone and handed it to me. Buddy lay asleep on his back on a bed, presumably Laney's, with his front legs stuck through a hot pink bra that was stretched across his chest. He looked like a drunk college kid, half undressed and out cold. Meghan recovered enough to say, "Looks like Buddy had quite the evening," before letting out another burst of laughter. This time, Laney joined her.

Skye flushed nearly as pink as the bra. I guessed that she was embarrassed that her uncle saw a bra and her mother was laughing loud enough for other tables to look at us. I remembered my own days as a twelve-year-old, always embarrassed by my parents. I rolled my eyes at Skye, pleased that, for once, I beat her to it. She returned the gesture, only more exaggerated. Skye won the eye-roll contest. That girl had talent.

We paid the bill and were waiting outside for the Rover car when Laney's phone buzzed. She looked down and gasped. "Oh my God, we have to get home right away."

"What happened?" I asked.

"My smoke detector just alerted me to a gas leak in the house and called 9-1-1."

We scrambled into the Rover car as it pulled up. I'd like to think I used my special Rover engineering team status to shift it into emergency mode to help us rush home, but our lawyers still wouldn't let us launch that feature. I couldn't even convince them to permit my idea of keeping it as a pilot only for the engineering team.

When we pulled up to Laney's house, three fire trucks stood outside with their lights flashing and firefighters milling around. A crowd had gathered nearby as Laney's neighbors took advantage of the commotion to check out their own local community reality show. We argued our way past a few firefighters to reach her front door.

Buddy lay on his side in the middle of the living room, seemingly fast asleep. He wouldn't let a squirrel run on the backyard lawn without barking at it, so I couldn't understand how he'd sleep through this home invasion.

A firefighter approached us. Tall and well-built, he had a sparkle in his eyes as he took his helmet off and unbuttoned his heavy fireproof jacket. "This your house?"

"Yes," answered Laney, her eyes wide as she looked at the veritable army of first responders.

"Well, ma'am, your dog is quite, uh, enterprising," said the firefighter.

Laney's eyes narrowed as she focused on his words. "What did Buddy do now?"

"Well, ma'am, as best we can tell, he broke out of that crate." He pointed to the large dog crate where Laney kept Buddy whenever she left him alone. "And then we think he jumped up and turned on the gas on your stove. Eventually it knocked him out."

"How'd he open the crate? I know I secured it before we left," Laney insisted.

"His paws must be quite dexterous. I've heard of dogs that can use their paws almost like hands." The firefighter pointed to Buddy, who had started moving a little. "He's pretty clever, for a dog." He shot an admiring glance at Buddy, who took up half the living room floor.

Laney's mouth had dropped open.

The firefighter continued, "One of your gizmos called in the alarm. Pretty slick, if you ask me. It called us, unlocked your door, and even told us it did that so we wouldn't break down the door. I might have to get me one of them." He looked ready to jot down the product specs or do a commercial endorsement.

A second firefighter, following the direction of Laney's glare, didn't seem as impressed with Buddy. "If it were me, I'd get a new dog before you need a new house."

Skye stepped toward him to defend Buddy. "This is our new dog. Uncle Marty got him for us."

All heads turned toward me.

Feeling the pointy tips of the daggers that Laney's eyes were throwing my direction, I took a step back.

"You! I blame you. You did this. You should take that … that dog." Laney avoided cursing in front of her daughter, although not by much.

"Hey, it's not my fault he turned on the gas," I defended myself.

"I didn't say it was your fault, I said I was blaming you. You can take him home." Laney tried to step toward me before remembering that her foot in a cast made her less mobile.

Judging the distance between me and the crutches under her arms, I took another step back.

"No, Mom!" Skye cried out. "We can't get rid of Buddy." She knelt down to hug the overgrown puppy, who was starting to revive. He tried to get to his feet but settled for a hug.

I agreed. I didn't think the pet delivery service accepted returns. And my apartment didn't allow pets. At least, I hoped it didn't.

Laney took another look at all the people in her home, sucked in a deep breath, and said, "We'll talk about this later."

Accepting this reprieve, I grabbed Meghan's hand and waved goodbye to Skye. It would be safest for me to leave while there were witnesses around. Buddy was on his own.

5

Monday Morning

"Dead?" asked Scott, the fourth member of our poker group that I'd reached already this morning.

"Yeah. It's hard to believe, but I found him on a hiking trail in the Santa Cruz Mountains on Saturday."

"You found him?" Scott's voice sounded like he found this as unlikely as I had. "Larry went hiking? Wait, you were hiking too?" Scott sounded even more surprised to hear this.

"Yes," I sighed. "It's a long story. The cops didn't want me to tell anyone until this morning ..." Fighting my sense of déjà vu, I proceeded to tell the story of finding Larry yet again.

I'd caught the earliest flight to Portland this morning so I could crash Raj's meeting with Doug Samerson. Meghan had flown off on her own business trip to New York for the week, so at least that timing had worked well. Yesterday, Raj told me he hadn't been allowed to talk about the meeting. Apparently, Samerson had asked to meet with a star engineer from Rover. Not a surprise that Raj had been selected, everyone knew Raj was one of our rock stars.

As I finished catching Scott up to date, he asked, "When's the funeral again?"

"There's a short memorial service tonight at his next-door neighbor's house. I don't know when the funeral will be. It's at 7:00, okay?" I was tired of repeating the same conversation over and over.

"Oh, tonight?" Scott paused. "I can't make it tonight, but let me know when the funeral is and I'll be there."

"Scott, come on. It's for Larry. Skip your other thing," I said as I got out of the Rover car in front of Sirius Innovation's Portland offices.

"I can't. Sam got us Warriors tickets for tonight." He added, "Second row," as if that justified skipping out on his friend's memorial service.

I didn't tell Scott that he just nailed Sam for lying to me about having a customer dinner tonight that he was obligated to attend. Perhaps it shouldn't have surprised me. I rarely saw most of the guys in the poker group outside of our games. I wasn't going to beg Scott. "Okay, catch you later."

All the guys had been shocked and saddened to learn of Larry's death, but only Drew told me he'd join me tonight at Larry's shiva.

Shaking my head, I tried to put the rest of them out of my mind. I needed to focus on today's meeting at Sirius. Larry had worked with these people, or at least they all worked at the same company. Perhaps someone would know why Larry had gone hiking. Or if Gloria had threatened him recently?

Raj was waiting for me in the lobby. I was glad he'd apologized and had a good excuse—I didn't want to lose him as a friend. I didn't have that many at work, which wouldn't have surprised Meghan. She'd learned I only knew the names of a handful of my coworkers despite working at Rover for almost two years. Yet I only found out last month that they celebrated each month's birthdays in the break room. With cake. For everyone. But no one had ever invited me. They weren't an outgoing bunch.

"Good morning, Marty. I hope we do not have to peel any pineapples today." Raj smiled as he pointed at my shirt.

I had started our friendly competition by using as many wacky idioms as possible when we talked. Over time, I'd had to work harder to stay one step ahead of Raj's growing mastery of colloquial American English. He delighted in throwing crazy expressions back at me and seemed to spend more time researching unusual ones than I did.

I looked down at my shirt in confusion. The pineapples on it were already split in half, shining golden yellow against the blue background. I raised an eyebrow and looked sideways at him, a bit dubious.

Pleased with himself for stumping me with a bizarre saying, Raj said, "It is from Brazil. It means to tackle a problem or solve an issue." He grinned in triumph.

It wasn't enough that Raj beat me with American idioms. Now he had to go international.

Raj's clothing choice today—a navy-blue blazer with a light blue, long sleeve dress shirt and beige slacks—surprised me. Like most engineers, he almost always wore jeans. At most, long sleeve shirts or sweaters only made their appearance in winter. His fancy business attire made me a bit self-conscious.

Since I was joining Raj at this meeting without permission, I'd put a little effort into selecting one of my special Hawaiian shirts and making sure to wear clean jeans. I wanted to shine for my new bosses. They already might complain about me crashing their meeting with Raj, I didn't want them also annoyed at my clothing.

The shirt wasn't too ostentatious, more of a repeating pattern of pineapples on a dark blue background. The pineapples were bright, just like me.

We gave our names to the receptionist, who told us someone would be down soon for us.

I was surprised to be looking forward to meeting Samerson. It was probably envy. Along with some friends, Samerson had started his first company, an augmented reality software company, and sold it for a mint before he was thirty. He launched Sirius not even two months later as the venture capitalists in the Valley threw money at him. The company started as some robotics software effort before recently adding a new biotech division, where Larry had worked.

With a steady stream of glowing press, if not actual products shipping, the biotech division's goal was increasing human longevity. Samerson's strategy seemed a little ill-conceived to me—if robots took over all the jobs, how would people make enough money to afford to live longer?

While we stood to the side of the lobby, Raj and I watched the employees going into the building. It was nuts for Raj to have to fly to Portland to meet with a man who lived and worked most of the time only a few miles away from us in the Bay Area, but Raj explained this was Samerson's only open timeslot this month. Since Doug Samerson was about to buy our company, Raj did not mind the inconvenience.

I hated missing out on the *Star Trek* exhibition, but I wouldn't be able to look myself in the eye if I didn't do something to help figure out what happened to Larry when I had the chance. At least I could appreciate that my days weren't scheduled as tightly as Samerson's.

The receptionist called our names. A woman in her thirties, with a perfectly coiffed, bobbed haircut and an expensive-looking long sleeve dress, was chatting with the receptionist. The woman stood with her arms crossed against her body, rubbing them to stay warm even though the lobby felt comfortable to me. As we approached, she flipped a big smile onto her face before stretching out her hand. "Hi. We weren't expecting two of you, but we'll make it work. I'm Peri. Peri Syte."

I blinked in surprise, and she blushed. "Yes. My parents are biologists with a strange sense of humor." Recovering, she added, "I guess it was fate that I'm working at a biotech myself. Just call me Peri. I lead our People Power program."

Trying to recover from my poor first reaction, I said, "Power to the People," and raised a clenched fist.

Peri gave me a half smile with a small, forced laugh. "You must be Marty Golden. We weren't expecting you today ..." Her voice trailed off.

I jumped into the breach with the explanation that I had developed last night. "We thought it would be good for Mr. Samerson to meet two great engineers from Rover." Okay, it wasn't the most innovative excuse in the world, but it was all I could come up with.

Peri frowned and then shrugged. "It's fine, I guess. But you'll have to fill out all the visitor paperwork." She reached over to shake Raj's hand. "Nice to meet you. I'm in charge of talent acquisition at Sirius. I'm so excited to meet you ... both of you. Let's get you checked in so we can get going." She sounded far too excited to meet us than a normal person should. HR people must possess some special gene that enables them to fake excitement while toeing the company line.

I've visited plenty of companies for interviews, lunch with friends, and business meetings. Never have I seen such an elaborate process for guest entry. After completing a couple of forms and signing some documents, we had our pictures taken. Our pictures! While we waited for custom plastic photo badges to be printed, Peri kept up a steady patter of commentary about the advanced badging system deployed by Sirius.

Her bubbly voice was starting to annoy me. "... and all invented by Doug. I mean Mr. Samerson. He's so amazing," she gushed. "He wanted all our visitors to experience the amazing feeling of working here by receiving the same badge as employees. It actually allows you to badge into the building."

I wanted to wait until I had entered the building before asking about Larry, but I made a mental note not to drink any Kool-Aid that might be offered today. Did they really believe that using a badge to enter a building was such an exciting experience? I kept my mouth shut, as I wanted to make a good impression on the folks that might soon be in charge of Rover.

Noticing that she was still talking, I tuned in again and caught the tail end of her remarks.

"…a special souvenir for all our guests to remember their experience with us."

"Sort of like Disneyland," I added before I could stop myself.

Her eyes narrowed a bit, although she maintained her upbeat tone. "Sure." She paused, rubbing her arms again while we waited. When the guard gave the go-ahead, she leaned over and signed her name on the final form with large, looping letters and a heart drawn above the "I."

Not wanting to annoy my soon-to-be new head of HR before the merger even took place, I didn't make fun of her. At least not out loud.

She finished and said, "Okay, it looks like everything is set. Let's go have some fun!"

Raj leaned over and whispered to me, "She must be a fan of Universal Studios." He glided away as I tried to squelch a snort.

Peri must have heard something, because she glanced at me, eyebrows raised in a questioning arch. Raj was smooth. He snuck in his comment, yet I got caught. She didn't comment further as we experienced the joy of placing our badges on the reader and stepped through the opening.

As we waited for the elevator, Peri turned to us—or, rather, to Raj. "Have you heard our corporate slogan?" Without waiting for a response, she answered, "'Sirius Innovation. We're serious about innovating.' Isn't that clever?" She laughed and, again without waiting for a response, continued, "Mr. Samerson came up with that slogan too. He's so brilliant, isn't he?"

Raj and I both kept polite smiles on our faces as we followed her onto the elevator.

*****

From the brief tour of their offices, we confirmed that offices everywhere were equally boring. All I had resolved thus far was that Peri had heard of Larry's death but refused to talk about him further because of "employee privacy." After rows of cubicles, we stopped outside an area against the windows with several closed-door offices. We'd reached our destination: Exec-Land. I hoped this would be exciting, as it represented our Tomorrowland, after all.

"Have a seat," said Peri.

I sat on the low, pale green object that she indicated.

"You're meeting Vince first. All the engineers report up to him." She stepped over to ask the administrative assistant a question.

The object, with a pale green square along with a triangle-shaped piece of wood that reclined at an unusual angle, only resembled a chair. It almost met my criteria for a chair. Passing my minimum chair standards typically required padding, comfort, and four legs rather than the three on this object. Perhaps I'd mistaken where she pointed and sat on a coffee table by mistake?

Before she returned, I'd almost lost feeling in my right leg. I rubbed it only to feel the same sensation begin in the left leg.

"Oh, aren't those the most amazing chairs?" asked Peri. She'd reappeared without a sound. "I plan to buy some for my own home. Doug selected these on a European vacation and ordered them for all our executive waiting areas."

She kept up her running commentary on the awesomeness of

Sirius. I learned the chairs were avant-garde because Peri told us they were. I wasn't quite sure what defined an avant-garde chair but concluded it meant uncomfortable. I was learning a lot on this trip, except for what happened to Larry.

Wondering how long this would take and whether I could still make the *Star Trek* exhibition, I stood to stretch, then glanced at my watch and took a calming breath. I couldn't miss my flight since I had to escort my niece Megan home and make it back in time for Larry's service. But I still had plenty of time. I checked my phone again, forgetting that Meghan hadn't landed in New York yet. No message from Mace either. He and the Santa Cruz Sheriff's deputies must have still been following up on my leads.

As two men walked out of Vince's office, Peri looked up with a hopeful expression. Her face reddened when she saw them.

The shorter and more overweight of the two men paused outside the door. A badge reading "Clyde" dangled from his untucked white dress shirt that ballooned out from his jeans. He glanced at his watch, revealing a black and white watch band with an unusual pattern of stripes and dots. The fashionable design looked out of place on Clyde's otherwise frumpy presentation. Indicating a small stack of electronic gear in his hands, he asked his colleague, "Would you mind dropping these at my desk? I'm late for another meeting."

The other man, lanky with a runner's build and slicked-back black hair, nodded and reached out to grab the equipment. He too wore an unusual, yet similar, watch band with bright orange patterns. Taking the gear, he turned, then noticed the three of us. "Well, hello there, everyone," he said with a broad smile.

Raj jumped up and extended his hand in greeting. "Hello, my name is Raj. I am very honored to meet you. I am an engineer at Rover and am looking forward to our merger with Sirius." Raj must have been nervous about today's meeting too.

The man shifted his gaze to Raj and crinkled his forehead in confusion. "Well, good for you."

Realizing the man couldn't shake his hand with his arms full of gear, Raj lowered his hand and, with a curt nod, returned to his seat.

Peri smiled and, with an awkward gesture, waved her arms out to include me along with Raj. "They're visiting from Rover. This is Alan. He's our Sorcerer of Security."

Alan smirked, then gave a wink and slight bow to Peri before puffing out his chest and walking off, wires dangling behind him.

Peri reddened from the excessive display of manliness, then turned to the other man. "Clyde, do you know where Vince is?"

Clyde straightened and pasted an ingratiating smile on his face. "That dress looks great today, Peri. The people business must be treating you well." His smarmy charm oozed out and threatened to get all over my shoes.

Peri stepped back and crossed her arms as her voice went flat. "Clyde, I'd like you to meet Raj and Marty, two of the engineers from Rover. They're here to meet with Vince and Doug." She repeated, "Do you know where Vince is?"

A sour frown spread over Clyde's face. "How should I know? Tell him his system upgrade needs more work." He saw Raj fingering his new badge and snorted. "You tell him he should focus on securing our network rather than his damn pretty badges that don't work—"

Peri interrupted him with introductions. "This is Clyde. He's our Information Impresario."

Raj scrunched his eyebrows in confusion. "Excuse me, you are what?"

"I'm the damn IT guy," Clyde answered, and walked off. From behind, we could tell his thinning brown hair needed a cut, as it puffed out around his ears.

Peri tried to ignore his rude behavior, amping up her positivity through force of will. "We've given all our executive staff more whimsical titles to reflect our corporate value of 'Winning While Having Fun.'"

She took my bored nod as encouragement and continued, "Mr. Samerson bought his whole executive team new watches to reinforce our corporate value of 'Winning Over Time.'" Even she couldn't restrain a giggle at this nonsense. "I think his wife just liked the custom-designed watch bands that she found at some art fair."

She rubbed an empty wrist through her sleeve. "Mine is teal. It's home today. I walked around San Francisco all day Saturday with my husband. We got a little more sun than expected."

"It is important to know your values." Raj nodded at his own sage advice.

I jumped in to show her I wanted to be a team player too. "What are the other values?"

Peri looked surprised that I'd asked. "Another value is 'Winning Together.' We showcase this by having our entire exec team travel together with Doug as often as possible. That's why we're all in Portland today, together, and we'll fly home tonight. Together." Her excitement seemed to dim.

Raj said, "Winning is good."

Even Peri couldn't think of anything to add to this comment, so she left us to search for the elusive Vince.

I headed to the restroom. When I returned, Raj had already gone inside. I walked in and introduced myself to Vince, then asked, "Did you know Larry Cohen?" No sense in beating around the bushes; I was tired of all the HR-speak and wanted to make some progress.

"Who?" Vince seemed confused.

Before I could explain, the door swung open again and Peri popped in.

"Oh, good, I see you've found our Connoisseur of Code."

"Peri, give it a rest with the silly titles," said Vince.

She flushed but powered on. "I'm so sorry." She looked at Raj and then me. "Mr. Samerson has an unavoidable emergency that he has to deal with. He won't be able to meet with you today after all."

I tried to look on the bright side of things. "Oh well. I guess I'll have a chance to stop by the *Star Trek* exhibition after all before I head home."

Vince said, "Oh, that one at OMSI? It's great." He and I shared a nod of appreciation for the finer things in a geek's life. Then, with a sad shake of his head, he added, "But today's Monday. The museum's closed on Mondays."

My mouth dropped open.

Breaking the silence, Peri added, "Well, we do have some good news. We moved another meeting so Mr. Samerson can meet with you tomorrow back in our Palo Alto offices."

"I thought we had to fly here because this was his only opening for a month?" I grumbled, my frustration with the whole day spilling over.

Pasting an obviously fake smile on her face, Peri replied, "Well, yes, that had been the case, but now he has time open tomorrow. Isn't that wonderful?"

At least I could take Megan back home and make Larry's memorial service tonight. I'd hate to spend another day in Portland pretending to feel special.

Vince didn't even spend ten minutes with us before asking Peri to escort us back to the lobby. She kept up a steady patter on additional amazing aspects of Doug Samerson and Sirius Innovation. Her ability to memorize all the ridiculous marketing bullets and generate fake enthusiasm was impressive, if a bit creepy.

Today had been a total fiasco—no progress on Larry, no *Star Trek* exhibition, and confirmation that I was not considered the star engineer at Rover. All I got out of this trip was a commemorative badge. Although today's experience at Sirius had been far from magical, Peri was right—I wouldn't forget it.

6

Monday Afternoon

Megan sat in the aisle seat on the plane. It seemed best for me to take the middle seat to avoid subjecting someone else to a few hours of unfettered Megan-ness. She was an energetic eight-year-old with very strong opinions. Although she might have been seven? Or nine? I kept forgetting to ask Laney. To be more accurate, I kept chickening out of asking Laney how old my niece was. Anyway, I'd read somewhere that middle seats were safest in a plane crash. I justified my abandonment of Megan to the more dangerous seat by deciding that she'd be able to escape out of the plane faster from the aisle in case of a water landing.

Raj had switched his flight and left hours ago. Megan, however, couldn't return until the afternoon from the Oregon coast, where she'd spent the weekend with her cousins. So, I hung around the airport, finishing an important demo for work and texting with Meghan in New York. She commiserated with me about the wasted trip while I fretted that neither Mace nor the Santa Cruz deputies had called me back yet with an update on their investigation. Needless to say, in my gloomy mood, my productivity didn't break any records.

Megan's big hug and burst of frantic energy helped me snap out of my funk. Laney's sister-in-law had merely waved as she dropped off Megan outside the departures entrance, no doubt relieved that her own kid wasn't as big a handful. Of course, I'd only seen Laney's husband's family at her wedding, when the girls were born, and again at his funeral a few years ago. Maybe I should have added them to my holiday card list, if I ever remembered to send holiday cards.

Concentrating on convincing myself that the flight would be fine and that the pilots would do a good job because they didn't want the plane to crash either, I visualized a safe landing. If all went well, I'd get to Larry's service right before it started. I wasn't paying attention to the flight attendant's announcement as we taxied away from the gate until I heard laughter echo throughout the cabin. I stopped obsessing about possible sources of airplane failure and listened.

"... The other attendants will be passing through the cabin to make sure your shoes, socks, and purses match."

Megan leaned over to whisper, "What if I don't have a purse? Will they give me one to match my sneakers?" She stuck out her glittery sneakers while raising her left eyebrow and quirking her lip.

The attendant continued, "The other ladies and I would certainly not have shown up for work tonight if we had anticipated a sudden decompression during flight. However, if one does occur, then yellow masks will drop from the compartment over your seat. To start the flow of oxygen, you first have to stop screaming."

Megan elbowed me and we both smiled. I relaxed my death grip on the armrest a bit. I knew I could grab it again to help hold the plane together if turbulence struck, and I probably had some duct tape stashed in my backpack for a true emergency.

Laughter rolled through the cabin as the announcement continued, "For those of you traveling with a child—why? And for those of you traveling with two or more children, what on earth were you thinking? When the masks fall, first put the mask on the nicer child. That's the one who will take care of you when you're old."

Megan leaned over. "Would you give me or Skye the mask first?"

I didn't hear the rest of the announcement as I scrambled to think of a response. "You're both old enough now to put on your own masks, so I wouldn't have to choose." To avoid ruining my successful gambit, I managed to maintain a straight face.

Megan smiled at me when the announcement ended. "She was funny." She started to say something else but was interrupted by the attendant returning to add, "Oh, and by the way, this is a Boeing 737."

Megan grunted before turning to me. "What are you going to be for Halloween?"

Before I could respond that I had no idea, the attendant again added, "With 175 passengers."

Megan gave an exaggerated sigh as she crossed her arms. "She talks a lot."

Once again, the attendant interrupted my response. "Flight time is listed as two hours, but it's really an hour-fifty."

Apparently falling into the role of a comedy club audience member, Megan began to heckle the no-longer-funny attendant. "Hey! We're trying to talk back here."

We were sitting far enough from the front that the attendant didn't hear Megan—a good thing, as I'd hate for my seat to be shifted out to the wing.

We took off without further incident. As my nerves settled into their normal high state of concern that heavy metal objects had no business staying up in the air, I released the grip on the armrest. That is, until war broke out across the aisle.

Two high school-aged girls sitting by themselves had stuck green straws from their Starbucks cups into their mouths, taken out a deck of cards, and pulled down their seat trays. Within seconds, they'd immersed themselves in the most aggressive, fast-moving game of cards I'd ever seen. Elbows were flying, long hair flashing as their heads swung from side to side. I had to look away as their tension made my blood pressure rise. Flying already made me more nervous than a long-tailed cat in a room full of rocking chairs.

Megan craned her head to the side and watched with fascination, unconsciously twitching her hands and arms in sync with the girls. What would happen next? Would they use the straws to attack each other once they'd shredded their cards? I didn't know if I needed to reach for my flotation device or mask.

Mesmerized, Megan chewed up and down on a non-existent straw of her own. At one point, during a failed shuffling attempt, the cards went flying. Or perhaps they'd switched to 52-card pickup. Megan popped out of her seat to help gather the cards. Glad that I didn't have to sit next to the girls, I pulled out my computer to go over my presentation.

Megan wound up sitting in the aisle seat next to the two girls and joined in their next game. They must have chosen a slapping card game, like Egyptian Ratslap, as their playing got wilder. Squeals sounded as hands got slapped and arms slammed on the seat-back table. A cup of water spilled. The girls yelled, "The cards, the cards," and scrambled to pick them up before they got wet.

After more than a few passengers turned around to give them the stink eye, a flight attendant came over to quiet the girls. She told Megan to return to her seat.

Megan plopped down next to me and grumbled, "I don't like flight attendants. They're bossy. And they talk too much."

About an hour before we landed, another announcement came over the intercom. It wasn't the standard "return to your seat" or "look out your window at the smoke from the latest forest fire." Using her professional, calm voice, the flight attendant asked,

"There's no cause for alarm, but is there a doctor or nurse on board?"

Her announcement caused me to become alarmed. My heart rate shot up and my death grip resumed. I whipped my head around, trying to find the source of the disaster. Could a fast-moving killer virus attack the whole plane and bring it down when the pilots succumbed?

As a man and woman in front of us stood up, I shook my head. I had to stop watching late-night movies. The man, buff and big, looked like a former athlete. The attractive woman with him had an infant sleeping in a baby holster on her chest and looked almost too fit to have given birth recently. They walked up a few rows to where the flight attendants were clustered.

Leaning over Megan to watch, I guessed he'd been a high school jock before doing well in college, getting his medical degree, and marrying the pretty nurse. *Some guys had all the luck.*

The couple kneeled down in the aisle to examine what appeared to be a teenager slumped in his seat. They spoke to him and his mother while checking his pulse and eyes.

Seeing them consult in quiet voices helped me calm down. If a killer virus were on the loose, they would have been more concerned, horribly disfigured, or even dead already. More confident that things were under control, I loosened my clasp on the armrest. A little.

"Hope the doctor can help that kid," I whispered to Megan. I needed to get back home for Larry's service, not waste the evening getting diverted to some tiny airport in southern Oregon.

The baby in the woman's holster woke with a cry. She said something to her husband, who hurried back to their seats, grabbed a pacifier from the diaper bag, and stuck the binky in the baby's mouth. A moment later, she spoke to him again. He stood and rushed back to their seats, returning this time with a small medicine bag that he handed to the woman.

I'd had it backwards. My dad had often quoted me that old line about "When you assume, you make an 'ass' out of 'u' and 'me.'" Taking an EpiPen out of the small medicine kit, the female doctor stuck it into the boy's thigh. She and her husband, the nurse, crouched by the boy's seat, talking quietly to him.

I froze. My grip tightened again as I realized I'd forgotten something else important about Larry. Because of his allergies, he always carried an EpiPen in a pouch on his waist or in his backpack. He used to call it his "Epi-Pack" since people confused it with a fanny pack. He wasn't wearing one when I found him in the forest, and I hadn't noticed anything near him.

I'd never known Larry to go anywhere without his EpiPen. What happened to it? Had the squirrels started trading EpiPens for acorns? Larry wouldn't have gone hiking by himself very early on a Saturday morning and forgotten his EpiPen. That wasn't Larry, neither the hiking nor the forgetting. Since Larry's car was still parked in his driveway, someone must have gone with him to the hiking trail. Had that someone taken his EpiPen? I wondered if EpiPens had GPS tracking devices like smartphones and cars.

Another thought struck me. Had that someone killed Larry? Startled, I sucked in a deep breath.

I sat there in shock, staring vacantly into space as scenes from the forest and campground flitted through my brain. After some time passed, somewhere between thirty seconds and thirty minutes, applause jolted me back to my senses. The doctor stood and stretched. With a curt nod and small wave, she acknowledged her appreciative audience before leaning over to talk to the boy and his mother again. As the show ended, Megan used her elbow to push me away from her seat so she could have her space back.

I had to call Sergeant Jackson again—the police needed to understand that Larry would have had his EpiPen with him. I needed Mace's help to get the deputies moving and figure out who had killed Larry.

For the first time, I wondered whether Mace would even have access to the case details. TV show cops never seemed concerned that their jurisdiction didn't apply. If the heroes wanted to get involved, they simply nosed their way into a case. I'd annoyed the Santa Cruz County Sheriff's deputies too much to ask them for anything. For Larry's sake, Mace would have to intercede on my behalf. Partners did that for each other.

The doctor and nurse walked back to their seats. As they neared their row, the doctor was in mid-rant: "... left it at TSA security? Security should have tracked them down to give it back to him. His mother shouldn't be allowed to have kids if she can't keep track of his life-saving drugs."

The man merely nodded and said, "Mm-hmm."

I realized I could help Mace out by securing an expert's opinion before reporting my findings to him. The deputies might not have noticed the unusual sunburn on Larry's hand and arms, and they didn't know about his strong allergies. They'd kicked me out of the Girl Scout campground before I'd had a chance to show them the pictures from the tricorder app. This was a perfect opportunity for a doctor to give me and my partner her expert opinion on what killed Larry. Mace would impress his colleagues by having new information without even seeing the body and before the autopsy was completed.

Before the couple started to maneuver back into their seats, I popped up. "Excuse me, that was awesome."

At my compliment, the couple paused and mumbled thanks.

Before I'd fully formulated my thoughts, I launched into my request. "Would you mind looking at this picture of my dead friend?" I rotated my phone so the doctor could see Larry's body in the infrared photo. "I took it with this tricorder app and I'm trying to figure out—"

The woman recoiled, her face contorting into a grimace as she interrupted me. "John, can you make this stop?" She swiveled her glance to her husband.

John puffed out his chest and, with a threatening tone, said, "Hey. Stop bugging my wife."

I pulled back my outstretched arm. I'd succeeded in catching her attention, although perhaps I could have broached my request with a bit more diplomatic tact. Doctors probably didn't enjoy seeing pictures of dead people any more than normal folks did.

She nodded at his words with grim satisfaction and proclaimed, "I'm going to wash my hands and change her diaper." Without glancing in my direction, she tilted her chin up and strode off to the back of the plane, ignoring the admiring comments along the way. Super-Doctor-Mom needed to get ready for her next challenge.

When his wife had left earshot, John's face softened as he gave me a sheepish shrug. "Sorry about that." Then he leaned in closer. "You've got pictures of a dead guy using that new tricorder app? Man, I was going to get that app. Can I see 'em?"

When he saw the images, he was dutifully impressed.

Pointing to the sunburn on Larry's arm, which looked even more blotchy with white dots in the ultraviolet image, I asked, "He worked in an office all day and he was dead by mid-morning on Saturday. How could he get a bad sunburn that fast?"

John zoomed in for a closer look, swiping back and forth between the shots. "Was the body in the sun when you found him?"

"No. I found him in the middle of a forest, in a shaded area." I didn't mention my vomiting. "How could he get sunburnt after dying? Everything stops when you're dead, so …" My voice trailed off, as I didn't know where I was heading. My knowledge of medicine was limited to knowing how to put on a Band-Aid, take a pill, and watch a doctor on television.

John understood what I was asking anyway. "The cells in the

skin produce melanin for a little while after death, so a dead body could still get tan. I read about this in nursing school." He looked up and cleared his throat before adding, "I was kinda into post-mortem forensics for a while. Thought I might be a medical examiner." He handed the phone back to me. "The autopsy should determine the cause of death, but ..."

I'd never spent much time watching medical shows—way too much blood and gross stuff. I liked the crime series better, or the PI ones where the hero caught the bad guys by outsmarting them. Of course, I'd also always loved good sci-fi—to be honest, I liked bad sci-fi too. I blinked as I realized that John was staring at me with a quizzical expression. How long had I disappeared this time? "Sorry."

John asked, "I asked if he was highly allergic?"

Embarrassed, I only nodded in response.

"Well, maybe it's not a sunburn. I'd guess those could be hives or a skin rash and he died of anaphylaxis."

I got excited that I might have stumbled across something important. "He carried around an EpiPen all the time." Then, I remembered that it wasn't on the trail with him. "Well, almost all the time."

John quirked his lips. "It would have been good to have one with him when this happened."

I nodded sadly. John could really shut down a conversation.

Before I could ask anything else, John blurted out, "Oh." His tone changed as he looked over my shoulder. "She's coming back. We gotta stop talking and you should sit down."

I sat down and opened my magazine before the doctor returned to her seat. I stared at the pages with unseeing eyes as my mind raced from John's comments. Had Larry died from anaphylactic shock? Where was his EpiPen? Did anything else strange besides sunburns happen to dead bodies? I'd have to look that up later.

As we were landing, Megan brought up her hand to shield her

mouth from the row in front of us and whispered, "I don't want to be a nurse anymore."

She'd succeeded in pulling my attention back from my morbid thoughts. "Why not, honey? It's pretty cool how he helped out that sick kid. Just last month, you saw how the nurses helped your mother in the hospital and you decided that's what you wanted to be."

"I know, but now I want to be a doctor. They get to be in charge. That's more me."

7

Monday Evening

Shaking my head in disgust, I paused on the walkway leading to Carmela's porch. On my ride from the airport, I had heard from Drew, the last member of my poker group, who called to tell me that he hadn't been able to leave San Francisco in time for the service. Then, I'd babbled my way through a voicemail message to Mace.

An adult man shouldn't have such difficulty leaving a voicemail. I had no problems talking to people in person. *Mostly.* Since my challenges in leaving coherent voicemails for Mace last month, I'd focused on this. In the same way that I've tackled many of my failings, I looked online for tips on how to leave the perfect voicemail. Over the last month, practice had improved my skills to the point where messages I left for coworkers had me sounding like the head of a Toastmasters club. Yet, leaving one for Mace proved … so much harder.

Per my training, I'd started off well by stating my name and number in a clear, firm voice. After that, things spiraled south in a hurry. I got a little excited explaining how I took pictures of Larry's body in the forest, reminding him that Gloria might have taken him there, and explaining the emergency on the plane and what Nurse John had told me about Larry's possible allergic reaction. My message didn't truly get out of control until I'd started extolling the cool features of the tricorder app and recommended the San Jose Police Department buy it for officers.

Carmela's screen door banged open, again startling me out of my introspection. "Do you always stand around on the sidewalk staring at houses? That can be mighty suspicious, sonny. Better watch out or somebody'll call the police."

"I'm sorry …"

"Well, come on up here already. Everyone's here."

After I climbed the few steps to her door, the woman gave a friendly laugh and patted my shoulder. "Oh, that's all right. Come on in."

I followed her inside. When the screen door shut behind me, a dog in the back of the house started barking, and I flinched.

Carmela said, "Just ignore him. It's Larry's dog. I locked him up in a back room so he wouldn't go bothering nobody. I'll introduce you to everyone." With a slight limp, Carmela led me into her living room where a small group of people stood around, looking like they weren't quite sure what to do while they waited. "Everyone, this is Marty. Marty, this is everyone." She laughed again, the cackle of someone quite accustomed to amusing herself, and headed off to her kitchen, mumbling something about "more napkins."

A thin, bleached-blonde woman turned around from her conversation with a heavyset, bearded man and squealed, "Marty!" She rushed over and hugged me.

"Hi …" I was at a loss.

She pulled back to study me. "Oh silly, it's Lauren. Don't you recognize me?"

No. "Oh, sure, sorry. I almost didn't recognize you with the different hair." *And cosmetic surgeries.*

No one else seemed to be talking as they stood around watching us, each alone and yet pretending to be part of the group.

"It has been such a long time. Too long. My keto diet and aerial yoga have done wonders for me. Don't I look great?" She spun around with a smile and her arms extended to make sure everyone had a panoramic view.

"Like a different person." She certainly didn't resemble the girl I used to know. "I'm so sorry again about Larry. I wish I had the right words to say."

Her smile turned down as she patted my arm. "That's so sweet. I'm sure he's in a better place right now." Then her sad face disappeared as she snorted. "Well, at least a less messy place." She giggled and then noticed the heavyset bearded man who was approaching us. "Oh, I'm sorry, Rabbi. That wasn't very appropriate. I guess I'm just nervous. Larry and I weren't close, but still, it's a shock that he's gone."

"That's quite all right. Everyone has a different reaction to grief." The bearded man wore overalls with a faded flannel shirt, and spoke in a calm voice that matched his stride.

Lauren nodded. "It just puts everything in perspective. I mean, I could die too at any time, so, like, YOLO, right? I mean, I've got to live like there's no tomorrow."

The rabbi chose to ignore her comment and extended his hand to me. "Hi, Marty. I'm Rabbi Schneiderman. Thank you for coming." He held my hand softly between his large, callused ones and smelled like sunshine and fresh-cut grass. Although the beard seemed consistent, the rest of him was not at all the image of a bookish rabbi that I remembered from my youth.

"Sure …" I trailed off, not sure where to take the conversation from here. I didn't talk to clergy often and had no idea whether to talk about Larry or the weather.

The rabbi wasn't fazed. "Well, I'm glad you came. We had to rush to hold it today." He nodded toward Lauren. "Normally, I wouldn't even be here, but the regular rabbi and cantor were already busy tonight with other obligations. Fortunately, I was down here in the Valley running some errands, so here I am. I wasn't even sure if we'd have a minyan."

I glanced around the room, counting heads. Including me, we had nine in the house. A minyan for a Jewish service requires ten adults, although not all Jews were sticklers about this metric. I wondered which of these people were Larry's colleagues from work. I wanted to ask them if they knew if he'd gone hiking on Friday.

Unsure what else to say to a rabbi, I asked, "Uh, so you're not the regular rabbi?"

"Oh no. I left my position as rabbi a while back. I've become an organic farmer now. I'm into permaculture. Have you heard about it?" He perked up, taking a deep breath as if ready to launch into a detailed overview.

Trying to avoid a boring lecture, I asked, "Where's your farm?"

He released his breath. "Oh, I've got a small place way up in the Los Altos Hills. I only help out on Jewish ceremonies down in the Valley in a pinch." Rabbi Schneiderman paused as he re-checked the room. "Carmela," he called as she bustled past us, "we do still need a tenth person. Do you think Lawrence's neighbor on the other side could be persuaded to come over?"

"Goodness. No, I don't think so." Carmela shook her head adamantly. "Those two have not been getting along for a while now. Gloria'd get spittin' mad about his dog barking or ruining her bushes."

As if on cue, the dog barked again.

She shook her head. "Lordy, can she cuss." She blushed. "Oh, pardon me, Rabbi."

"It's okay. I've heard of cursing." He gave her a bemused smile, then scratched his head. "What can we do for our tenth person?"

I had an idea. That happened often, and some of them were actually good. Hollywood hadn't yet released a movie starring a problem-solving, engineer superhero. There was still time. "Rabbi, does the person have to be here physically?" I explained what I had in mind and he agreed it would work.

I texted my son, Eli. He was available, if not exactly excited. But college kids didn't typically have a lot of regular evening responsibilities. Partying didn't count. One of the few benefits available to a college student's parent was the ability to remind him or her who paid the bills. A few moments later, I had propped my phone on the chair next to me with Eli's face looking out at everyone. Proud of my solution, even if I didn't get to wear a fancy superhero costume or walk the red carpet, I gave a smug nod to the rabbi and he started the service.

Seeing my son's disembodied head chanting prayers on the seat next to me during a service for a dead friend felt bizarre. The rabbi didn't seem at all fazed as he shifted eye contact smoothly around the room, including Eli. Working with Silicon Valley types for years had acclimated the rabbi to creative uses of technology. He kept the service to the bare minimum, and when it ended, I said goodbye to Eli and joined the others in the kitchen to grab a drink and a small bite.

I checked with the other attendees only to learn that none of them were from Sirius. Strange that none of Larry's work friends had come. Had Larry been a loner too? And what was the deal with Gloria?

When I wandered over to the rabbi's homemade wine, one of the neighbors reached in front of me and took a glass, along with a flyer sitting next to the bottle. Curious, I picked up the flyer as well, then realized it was advertising the rabbi's produce delivery service. A highlighted section indicated that his crop of weed hadn't yet matured but would be available soon. Although I knew it was legal now, I wondered if marijuana was considered kosher. *Only in California.*

Almost before I could blink, Lauren had hugged me goodbye and the small crowd had melted out the door. My mother had taught me not to eat and run without helping clean up, so I stayed back. A bit embarrassed on behalf of the others, I asked Carmela if she needed any help getting her living room back in order.

"Oh, you're a dear. Perhaps if you could help carry these chairs back to Larry's house, then I wouldn't have to wrestle them back over there on my own."

I agreed and grabbed the chairs. After putting them away, I veered past Larry's car, still wondering how he had gotten to the forest. Pausing, I peered inside. Nothing remarkable—the inside looked like anyone's car. In fact, it was neater than most people's cars, with the front seat and floor empty. Surprised that a hoarder's car wasn't crammed with stuff too, I shifted to look in the back. Clear, but something was on the floor. I leaned over to examine it closer.

"Now don't you be touching nothing." Carmela's voice came from right behind me.

I jumped, nearly knocking her over. "Why?" I looked around, searching for danger.

"Just in case them police might want to dust his car for prints."

"I thought you said they weren't coming up here. And didn't we go in his house? Twice?"

"Well, now, that was different. We had company over. Where would everyone sit?"

Carmela must have watched the same crime shows that I did.

Using my shirt so I'd keep my fingerprints off his car, I tried the handle of the back door.

It was unlocked.

I pulled the door open and leaned forward. Carmela put her hand on my back as she craned her neck to see.

The strap of Larry's Epi-Pack lay on the back floor, poking out from under the seat right near the door, as if it had fallen off while he was getting out of the driver's seat.

I jerked back and then had to grab Carmela to keep her from falling. We took a few steps away from the car before catching our balance. "His EpiPen bag is in there," I explained.

"And that's why you plumb knocked me over?"

"I'm sorry. I didn't expect to see it there. That's evidence for the police." I had never expected to be the person who found Larry's EpiPen. I stood up a little straighter.

Carmela's eyes grew wide. "Well, that's mighty exciting news. Should I call 9-1-1?"

"I don't think that's necessary. It's not an emergency. I've been helping out the police already, so I'll let them know." Time to call Mace again.

Carmela seemed impressed and watched as I shut the door, again using my shirt. I didn't want to contaminate another possible crime scene.

After helping Carmela back into her house, I waited by the curb for my Rover car to arrive. I'd call Mace once I got away from the disconcerting feeling of Gloria's dark, empty house looming over me. I tried out my X-ray vision for the umpteenth time, but it was still on the fritz. Only a dark, empty house returned my scrutiny.

8

Tuesday Morning

I woke up Tuesday morning extra early and full of resolve. Visiting Larry's office at Sirius today could be a key step in figuring out what had happened to him. Learning my boss considered Raj the best engineer at Rover instead of me was also a kick in the pants. I'd always been a top performer, and my ego wasn't ready for a reset.

Determined to start setting the record straight, I got to Sirius's San Jose headquarters before Raj for our rescheduled meeting. I hoped to find someone who knew Larry and could help shed some light on the situation. My pointless victory only meant I got to sit around the lobby for a while waiting for Raj so we could check in together. No one approached me to talk about Larry nor did anyone pass by who looked especially guilty of murder. At least I managed to catch Meghan for a quick text exchange before she had to run for her next meeting. I should have used the extra time to work on my presentation. Or to sleep.

"Hope second time's the charm," I said as Raj walked up, planning to surprise him with an unexpected idiom and gain a small advantage in our never-ending contest.

"Yes, because three strikes and we're out," he responded with a broad grin as he one-upped me yet again.

Dang. Despite racking my brain, I couldn't come up with any stupid sayings built around the number four. I used to mine a rich vein of idioms from American sports that Raj didn't know. Clearly, he'd been studying. Another area where I was losing my edge. Today's meeting with Doug Samerson better take place. I wouldn't give three cheers if I had to come back a third time to meet a CEO with poor time management skills.

After checking in, we waited only a few minutes before the receptionist motioned us forward. A good-looking blond man wearing crisp slacks and a tailored shirt stood by the desk. He handed us business cards and introduced himself. "I'm Sean Peters. Peri is out this morning at a doctor's appointment, so I'll give you a short tour and bring you to Doug's office." His voice had a deep, resonant tone that sounded more practiced than natural. His card read, "Chief Cat Herder." I managed to avoid rolling my eyes. At least this had to be better than another dose of Peri's rah-rah enthusiasm.

As Raj shook his hand, he asked, "Does Sirius have a lot of cats?"

Sean let loose with a hearty chuckle. "Well, that's not really what I do. I'm the chief of staff for Doug Samerson. I do a little of everything, I'm afraid. I run the executive staff meetings, lead the corporate strategy reviews, and handle any projects that fall through the cracks. If all goes well, I expect to be running some of our new acquisitions soon."

Shocked, I took another look at him. He couldn't have been older than thirty. His comment threw me for a loop. Besides calling into question the intelligence of Sirius Innovation's CEO for putting such an inexperienced person in charge of a new acquisition, Peters needed to work on his diplomacy skills. Although he hadn't met us before, the first words out of his mouth were to brag that he'd be running our company. I swallowed any snarky comments and shook his hand. After all, despite how crazy it sounded, he might soon be in charge of Rover.

I pulled out my badge from yesterday and started to put it by the badge reader.

Sean smirked. "Oh, how cute, you brought your commemorative badge back." Dropping the condescending tone, he added, "Just flash it at the receptionist and follow me. Our badging system is, um, temporarily not working to its fullest potential."

Although we held up our badges, the receptionist may not have noticed them amidst a group of employees filing in along with us. She didn't seem to care. We hurried to catch up with Sean as he bypassed the elevators and headed for the stairs. Holding the door to the stairway for us, he said, "I'm into extreme sports and don't get as much exercise as I'd like during the week, so I try to take the stairs whenever possible. Come on, it's only four flights to the top." He bounded away up the stairs.

Raj and I looked at each other. He grinned at Sean's ridiculousness while I shrugged in resignation. We followed him up the stairs, although at a slower pace.

By the time I trudged up to the fifth floor, I'd started sweating. As Sean waited, holding the staircase door for me, I tried unsuccessfully to hide my puffing. Maybe Meghan had a point about my needing to get to the gym.

Raj waited beside Sean, not sweating though breathing harder than normal.

Peters let out another chuckle and gave me a jocular slap on the back. "Gotta get you taking the stairs more often, hey, buddy? Heart-healthy and all that." His teasing grin didn't feel quite as friendly as his words.

Competitive bugger, isn't he?

Hoping to slow Sean down long enough to catch my breath, I asked, "Did you know Larry Cohen?"

Peters gave me a curt nod as his grin faded. "Yeah."

It made sense. Sirius wasn't all that large, and there couldn't be too many employee deaths. Unless they made stair climbing mandatory.

In a flat, near-monotone, Peters said, "I was really busted up when I heard the news." Without further delay, he swiveled to head off across the floor.

The combination of his rah-rah attitude, extreme sports, and faking that he cared about Larry pissed me off. "If you were so close, why didn't you come last night?" I was still puffing as I followed him.

He didn't even turn his head. "I don't do religion."

I noticed he didn't have to ask what had happened last night. He had heard about Larry's shiva service even though no Sirius employees had attended. If he was the Chief Cat Herder, why didn't he encourage others to go? Or had he discouraged the other employees from attending? Curious now, I asked, "So you knew him well?"

Peters almost stumbled, his whole body tensing before he answered, "We were working together on a project when he ..." He came to a stop, turning and waving his arms in a half-shrug as his voice petered out.

My stomach fluttered. I hadn't expected that they actually worked together. "Really? You're a biologist too? What were you working on with him?" Before he could answer, I added an even more important question: "Did he mention anything late last week about going hiking in the Santa Cruz Mountains?"

"I really can't say." He looked away and crossed his arms, fidgeting as he glanced down the hallway.

"Can't or won't?" I spit out in my own anger. I didn't even know which question he hadn't answered.

"Now listen." Peters' voice grew strident and lost its deep resonance. He clenched his fists as he glared at me with a reddened face. "Our team was working on a strategic assignment that I can't discuss. I already told the cops everything they need to know. I don't have to explain myself to you."

I glared back. Larry was more than just a poker buddy. He was my friend, and I wanted to know what happened to him.

Raj cleared his throat, breaking the tension. "Um," Raj stuttered as he was struck by the combined force of both our glares. Recovering, he added, "I believe Marty only meant that he is very upset about the death of his friend and he wants to understand what happened. It is good that you have talked to the police."

In my anger, I hadn't registered Peters' words. If the deputies had spoken to him, then they must be looking into Larry's death. What did Peters mean by "everything they need to know?" What did he leave out? I knew Larry wasn't the type to go on hikes, especially ones that could kill him. There was more to his death. There had to be. Peters might not even realize he knew something important.

I took a small step back and tried to swallow my anger, which felt like it fell into a pit in my stomach. Looking Peters in the eyes, I rolled my shoulders back and raised both hands in surrender. Concentrating on calming down, I said, "Hey, I'm sorry. Raj is right."

Sean's glare eased and he unconsciously smoothed the front of his shirt, as if to wipe away the memory of our confrontation. "Okay," he said before clearing his throat. "Let's get you to Doug's office." His earlier baritone revived as he set off at a brisk pace.

Before following, I nodded my thanks to Raj, who raised his eyebrows as if to communicate, "Not a great plan to upset the guy who may soon be running Rover." As usual, Raj was right.

"What kind of extreme sports do you do?" asked Raj, changing the subject in an attempt to rescue today's visit.

The distraction worked. Sean slowed and brightened. "I like

wingsuit flying. You get to be like an eagle." His enthusiasm reignited as he proceeded to explain the sport to Raj.

As I followed them across the fifth floor, I resolved to avoid all team-building events if Sean wound up running Rover.

*****

"You ever been to the Cayman Islands?" Doug Samerson boomed yet another one-sided question at us. A slightly overweight man with a goatee that tried to make up for his thinning hair, he waved his arms a lot and projected his voice as if to make up for his short stature.

I'd spent the last five minutes staring at the pictures on his desk, his wall, and occasionally making eye contact while he yammered on about himself. For a meeting sold as a get-to-know-you session, apparently it should have been labeled a get-to-know-Doug meeting, as we had yet to do more than introduce ourselves. At first he seemed a little surprised to have a second visitor, but that hadn't stopped his monologue.

He continued, "We went a few weeks ago for a long weekend, down Friday and back on Sunday. I love it there."

Acting his normal, polite self, Raj kept attempting to interact. He gestured to the photo of Samerson with his family. "And did your wife enjoy it too?"

Samerson looked startled by the question as he hunched down in his chair. "What? No, she didn't go. I mean, I went by myself. She went to her sister's." He darted his eyes from side to side and repeated, "I went by myself."

To me it seemed awfully far to travel for a three-day trip, whether alone or with someone, but I didn't say anything.

Samerson recovered his equilibrium by returning to an obviously well-worn line. "Did they tell you why I named the company Sirius Innovation?"

We were back to being his audience for today's performance. Without looking at each other, we answered his question with a shake of our heads in unison.

Within the first two minutes, I'd concluded that Doug Samerson was a moron. Most of the CEO/founders that I'd met were wicked smart. Every once in a while, however, an idiot somehow got funded by the venture capitalists, or made it through the dog-eat-dog competition to the top. Now this top dog was about to eat another dog, Rover. Someone else must write Samerson's public speeches.

"It's because we're aiming high. Shooting for the stars." Samerson paused in his explanation and waited, flashing us a smug grin as he folded his arms over his ample stomach, now confident again as he watched for our reaction.

Neither Raj nor I understood what he was talking about.

After we didn't react, Sean Peters jumped in to explain. "Sirius is also the name of the brightest star in the sky. Get it? Aiming high? Shooting for the stars?" He and Samerson laughed, as if this was the funniest joke they'd heard all day.

Maybe it was.

In a rare moment of discretion, I didn't point out that Sirius was also known as the "Dog Star," so of course they should buy Rover. In my humble opinion, that would be an even funnier comment. Growing up, my dad had warned me about not making the boss look bad. He had forgotten to mention that most bosses managed to do that all by themselves, and that it was the workers' role to make their bosses look good. At least, that was how it seemed to work wherever I'd been.

When Samerson took a breath, I interrupted to ask my long-awaited question. "I understand you have a number of strategic initiatives underway in addition to the acquisition of Rover. Could you tell us about the strategic project that Sean was working on with Larry Cohen?"

"Was that the one with Larry, Gloria, and ..." Samerson glanced to Sean for confirmation.

Gloria!?

I started to speak, but Sean leaned forward, his eyes flashing with anger, and interjected, "I don't think we should discuss other strategic projects with our guests today since they're not employees yet."

Samerson's face grew puzzled for a moment before comprehension sank in. He stood up and turned to his whiteboard. "Well, without going into details I shouldn't reveal, let me explain my overall vision for Sirius."

Sean threw a frown in my direction and then turned his rapt attention to Samerson and the board.

I looked sideways to see Raj directing a raised eyebrow at me. He gave me a quick shake of the head.

I got the eyebrow-encoded message and nodded. I wouldn't do anything else to screw up today's meeting.

After five minutes of convoluted explanation had clarified nothing about the company's overall direction except confirming Samerson's incoherent thought processes, he got himself sidetracked and started telling personal anecdotes again. Perhaps fooled into thinking he had us mesmerized by his charisma, Samerson switched to humor. "When someone screws up when they work for me, do you know what I call them?"

Following Raj's eyebrow-influenced guidance not to speak, I shrugged and tried to look interested. I didn't dare look at Raj, not wanting to start laughing aloud at our new CEO.

"A taxi," was Samerson's punchline. He and Sean roared with laughter.

But ... You're buying a driverless car service.

Acting tough in front of the troops must have been Doug Samerson's definition of effective leadership. That was the kind of attitude that never inspired people to take risks for a company. Maybe I needed to update my resume again after all.

I forced a polite smile as I shifted in my seat and watched them laugh. Out of the corner of my eye, I caught a glimpse of gold. Adjusting my position as I pretended to laugh allowed me to get a better view. A door to the side of Samerson's office was ajar, the gleam of bright gold coming from what could only be a private bathroom.

He had a private bathroom? Made of gold? My eyes widened as I signaled Raj with my eyebrows to check out the ostentatious display in the corner.

Raj could talk in "Eyebrow," but despite understanding three other languages, he apparently couldn't read it.

We sat there for another five minutes while I tried to get Raj's attention, Sean sucked up to the CEO, and the CEO talked about himself. All in all, a typical meeting with senior executives. Before I knew it, Samerson had shaken our hands and we were following Sean back through the building.

The whole way back to the elevator and out into the lobby, Sean raved about Samerson's inspiration and vision, and he didn't appear to be faking his enthusiasm. I held it together long enough to shake his hand without calling his boss an idiot, or yawning.

As Raj and I found ourselves alone again outside the building, I slumped in exhausted relief on a bench. "Well, he certainly appeared smart from a distance."

"Your confusion is understandable. Light travels faster than sound, so some people only appear bright until you hear them speak." Raj laughed, and I joined in.

As we waited for the Rover car to arrive, my annoyance started to grow. After seeing Samerson's private restroom made of gold, I had figured lunch would be spectacular. Now, after the rapid exit, it was back to the office and a plastic tuna sandwich from the small café across the parking lot. Maybe I'd stop to buy a lottery ticket. My chances of striking it rich with stock options seemed about as likely as winning tonight's lottery drawing.

I considered what I'd learned from today's visit. First, despite wanting to be a brilliant, inspirational, visionary leader like Steve Jobs or Elon Musk, Samerson still played in the minor leagues. Second, gold bathroom! Finally, both Samerson's and Sean Peters' behavior had caused my highly-tuned detective's antennae to tingle.

I needed to talk to Mace Jackson. *And tell him what?* As I considered our time with Samerson and Peters, a detail started to come into focus. Unlike all of Samerson's direct staff, Peters didn't have a colorful watch band on his wrist or some ready excuse for not wearing it.

I got excited.

This was it!

I'd cracked the case. Peters must have lost his watch in the struggle when he killed Larry. That was why he grew so sensitive when I brought up Larry and didn't want to talk about their relationship. Maybe they'd become friends while working on that strategic project together and then had irreconcilable differences on the project's direction. As part of his extreme sports training, Sean lured Larry out on a Saturday morning hike and killed him on the trail when Larry wouldn't change his mind to support Sean's position.

It all hung together. The police just needed to locate Peters' watch on the trail and we'd have him for Larry's murder.

Would the police honor me with an award ceremony? Maybe the mayor would make me an honorary detective? I'd prefer a special costume ... or signal. Like Batman's Bat-Signal. Wait. Would San Jose or Santa Cruz County honor me? I groaned as I thought of the bureaucratic in-fighting that could take weeks to resolve and cost me my renown. Then, I smiled as I realized I could offer to attend ceremonies in both places. Did Santa Cruz County have a mayor? Maybe their council just met in the woods and ate granola.

Raj interrupted my thoughts. "Aren't you coming?" He was sitting inside a Rover car and looking up at me with a puzzled expression.

Shaking away my daze, I hopped in.

9

Tuesday Afternoon

Mace called me back! I answered on the first ring, fumbling my phone in my eagerness as I stood outside my apartment building with my nieces. "Hey, Mace... I mean Sergeant." I kicked myself for my mistake when I heard his annoyed grunt.

After our last case, he'd told me to use his title whenever we interacted in a professional situation. He'd said, "Call me Sergeant." Then, when I'd used his title and asked if I could do a ride-along in his police car someday, he'd added, "No, actually, don't call me. Period." I was sure he meant he'd call me to arrange the timing. Ever since, he must have been really busy.

"You've called me at least six times this week and it's just Tuesday," came Sergeant Mace Jackson's low rumble. Before I could respond, he rumbled on, "But the captain made me call you. I got volun-told to be the liaison for this investigation with the Santa Cruz County Sheriff's Office."

"Wow, so it's true? They started an investigation? Now they believe me about Larry? Did any of my tips pan out yet?" My heart started beating faster than my words spilled out as I paced on the sidewalk.

Earlier, I'd picked up my nieces from school for a quick visit with my neighbor, Mrs. Kim, who watched them occasionally. The girls had bonded with her, and her cookies and tea didn't hurt. Now, as I spoke on the phone outside my apartment building, Skye and Megan dropped their backpacks on the ground and crossed their arms. Megan's eyes narrowed, shooting laser beams in my direction as she gestured for me to follow her. Skye attempted her own version of airplane ground controller signals, trying to get me moving inside.

I had murder on my mind, so I shooed them away.

"Did they collect Larry's EpiPen from his car? Did they find any fingerprints? DNA? What about Gloria? Did they arrest her yet?" Despite hunching over and covering the mouthpiece, I was too excited to keep my voice down, and the girls could hear my side of the conversation.

The girls stopped their efforts at trying to get me into the building. Looking at me with wide eyes, they seemed torn between intrigue and fear.

I walked farther down the sidewalk, away from them. They were too young to get involved in something this sordid.

"I just said it's an investigation. I sure didn't say anyone believed you." Mace's staccato words seemed to struggle to come out of his mouth. Then he sighed heavily and, in a more resigned tone, added, "They're treating his death as suspicious. The autopsy isn't complete yet. Anyway, we can't share any details with you." He paused and muttered something under his breath before saying to me, "They want you to come in tomorrow morning to answer some questions."

I got to be his partner again. *Super-agent Marty is back!* "I'm in. I can take some time off and join the investigation—"

He cut me off. "You are not joining the investigation, only talking to the deputies about what you saw. This time you need to be polite, or you'll find yourself spending some time in our holding cell." His voice gained that intense tone that he used when he wanted to intimidate people. It worked.

I understood. He wanted me to be part of his secret investigatory unit, in case the Santa Cruz Sheriff's deputies were in on the conspiracy. This would be like that movie ...

I shook my head. This wasn't the time to get stuck in one of my sidetrack reveries. Mace needed to know the latest breaking news. "I think we have two new suspects. Doug Samerson, the CEO of Sirius Innovation, and Sean Peters, the Chief of Staff. Peters acted very suspicious today when I asked him about Larry. And he wasn't wearing one of those custom watch bands." I paused for breath.

"What?" The clipped tone had returned. He even grew a little strident. "You can't be going around accusing people of killing someone. If anyone is acting suspicious, it's you. And there's no 'we.' There's only you and me."

And we just disagree.

I had to stop finding lyrics to old songs in my daily conversations. Before I could speak again, Mace informed me when and where to show up before hanging up on me. I didn't even get a chance to explain my theory that Sean lost his watch on the trail during a struggle to the death with Larry. I still felt energized that the police had added me to their team. Tomorrow, I'd impress Mace and his Santa Cruz deputy friends with my observations and deductive reasoning.

Confident that all would be put to rights soon for Larry, I put my phone in my pocket and walked back to the girls. I felt an odd sense of elation to get confirmation that my friend's death had been deemed suspicious. Skye had her head cocked to one side and her mouth open to ask me to explain when a loud car roared up, music blaring, and skidded to a halt right in front of us.

A tall woman with wild, frizzy, ash-blonde hair popping out

of her Red Sox ballcap and blown wilder by the wind, sat facing us in a red convertible. "Cuz! How's things shaking? And who are those beautiful women hanging around with you? Don't they know better?" She sprang out of her low-slung car to screams of joy from the girls.

My cool cousin, Samantha, had arrived.

A psychologist from Boston who had grown up in Oklahoma, Samantha was in town for some convention. Laney and I had both offered her a place to stay, but she chose me because I was cooler. To avoid hurting Laney's feelings, she told us she didn't want to force the girls to double up while she was in town.

Samantha did some complicated hand gesture involving fist bumps, high-fives, and flickering fingers with Skye and then Megan before giving me a quick slug on the shoulder. Samantha didn't do hugs. Before I knew it, she threw their backpacks in the trunk, got the girls to jump into the tiny, rear-facing bench seat, and sat back down in the driver's seat. The girls hadn't seen her in over a year and already they were best buds again.

"Let's go, Cuz. Let's boogie over to Laney's. I'm starving. It's way late o'clock on my East Coast stomach."

I looked skeptically at the girls, crouched in the back and looking out the window. "Are there even seatbelts back there? Maybe we should take Rover."

"Oh, Marty, don't be such a fuddy-duddy. Get in already."

I texted Mrs. Kim that we'd stop by to see her another time and got in. Samantha had that way with people.

When I looked over my shoulder at the girls, Megan gave me a wide-eyed grin and a thumbs up while Skye pointed at her seatbelt and threw me an eye roll.

We zoomed off, music blaring as we blew past jealous people in boring cars. It was time to ride—ride like the wind.

*****

While we waited for dinner to be delivered, we sat around Laney's kitchen table talking. As a surprise for the girls, I'd ordered a special dinner from El Salvadore Restaurante. We'd discovered the restaurant by accident when the girls stayed with me last month while their mother was in the hospital. There had been a little incident that night, so I wasn't allowed back inside the restaurant, but ordering delivery wasn't breaking any rules. At least not in my book. Just to be safe, I placed the order in Laney's name.

Laney propped her booted foot on a chair while Samantha picked on me. "Girls, did you ever hear the story about when your Uncle Marty was young and wouldn't jump off a tall rock into a lake? Younger kids like your mom jumped right off, but nope, not your Uncle Marty."

Skye took the bait. "What happened?"

"He's probably still stuck up on that rock." The room filled with girl giggles.

Before I could defend myself, the stories devolved into a session of "Pick on Marty" as Samantha rolled out one after another. I tried to keep a frown on my face but it was hard in light of the constant laughter. Samantha was a funny storyteller, even if most of her stories were at my expense and exaggerated.

A quick conversational detour to discuss the girls' various Halloween costume options for Saturday left me adding a reminder to my calendar to get a costume for myself. Before I knew it, the conversation had switched gears, as usual, to yet another discussion about what color or pattern to paint Laney's new car.

For weeks, Laney had delayed finalizing the order of her replacement car for "Sunshine" while she and the girls debated the silly paint job. "Sunshine" was one of the last major items that Laney's husband had picked out with her and the girls before his death, which might have impacted her unwillingness to move on. But I was tired of hearing debates about car colors. The dealer had called a few times already to tell her that the car had been delivered and they could finish a custom paint job in a day if she'd tell them what color.

Everyone ignored my logical solution to paint it the same neon-yellow color as before, and they were debating the relative merits of pink versus orange when I'd finally had enough. "Okay, my turn. Here's a story about something Poppa did when we all went to Disneyland together."

Even though I hadn't suggested unicorns, rainbows, or some other paint option, everyone turned to listen to my story—probably only to see if it could beat Samantha's last one. The girls knew Poppa only as a grandfather, not when he was younger and more energetic.

"So, both our families were standing in line forever for a ride at Disneyland, and this payphone near us rings. Poppa answers it in a fake Russian accent and says, 'Lunar Base One. This is a secret number. You should never call again.' Then he hung up on them."

Laney, Samantha, and I all burst out laughing as we remembered that hot summer day.

Skye's face puckered in confusion. "What's a payphone? Is that like a burner phone?"

Megan asked, "Poppa speaks Russian?"

Without missing a beat, Skye answered, "He probably used that translation app."

Megan ignored her to ask, "Is Lunar Base One like the International Space Station?"

With an impish glint to her eyes, Skye then added, "I read they're going to build a lunar base soon."

"Poppa was an astronaut?" popped in Megan as she got into the game.

"Was space even invented back when you were young?" added

Skye with a malicious smirk, sure she got the best of us now since all three adults had gone silent.

She was punking me something terrible, so I was glad to jump up when the doorbell rang. I went to get the food and avoid more questions that made me feel old. I took the bag of food and set it on the ground so I could pay. When the delivery guy handed me his tablet for the thumb scan, I gasped.

Right above his wrist was a small tattoo of a hula dancer, just like the members of the drug gang from last month had. I snuck a peek at his face and almost swallowed hard.

He was one of the men who had been there that night.

I bent my head so he wouldn't recognize me. My hand shaking, I decided to add a big tip in case he did. Maybe this would work as a bribe to encourage him to forget he'd ever seen me. After all, I hadn't done anything to them. What happened hadn't been my fault. Not really.

Keeping my head down, I mumbled thanks and closed the door behind him.

Leaning against the door to avoid fainting, I felt a lump grow in my stomach as I started to worry if I'd make it home alive. Perhaps I had been naïve to assume they'd never bother me again. Was this driver even a regular delivery guy? Had they used their connections to track me down to my sister's house so they could send a disembodied head in the bag to scare me?

I grimaced and stepped away from the bag sitting on the floor. Then, I reconsidered. That plot was straight out of a scary movie.

Perhaps they had gone after my friend Larry to keep me from uncovering their conspiracy … Wait, that was another movie, not reality.

Who would even expect gang members to have day jobs? Housing costs had skyrocketed again, but did even drug gangs need to make extra money to afford living in Silicon Valley?

Now I had to worry about whether the driver had recognized

me and would tell the others. I didn't want the gang to know where I lived, but I also didn't want them thinking I lived here and put my sister and nieces in jeopardy. With a heavy heart, sour stomach, and holding the bag far away from me, I returned to the table.

The others loved their food. The girls showed off their black bean and rice volcanoes to Samantha, who used their plates to demonstrate how the Big Dig tunnels were built under downtown Boston back in the '90s. I toyed with my food, no longer in the mood for dinner. When a car brake screeched outside, I flung myself to the floor to avoid the bullets.

"Cuz, what are you doing?" Samantha asked. "You're acting as antsy as a Yankee fan during a Red Sox home game. And you didn't eat any of this delicious chow. Stop being a nervous ninny. What's the deal?"

The girls giggled as they watched me get up from the floor and sit back down.

"Nothing. I'm not hungry tonight." I tried to avoid flinching when another car drove past.

"Well, you're missing out. This is delicious. We have to go to this place sometime," said Laney.

I tried to figure out how to discourage this idea without revealing why.

Samantha noticed my flinching. "There you go again, acting all scaredy-cat. Maybe some ice cream will chill you out?" She added, "I have to get some mint chocolate chip anyway. I'm superstitious that way. Always eat the same ice cream on the night before a skydiving competition starts."

"What?" asked Laney.

"Skydiving?" I was puzzled. Maybe that was some weird psychology term, like generalized anxiety disorder.

"Of course." She shook her head in exasperation, as if this were obvious. "I'm in town for the annual skydiving convention. I'm competing Thursday. Tomorrow afternoon's a trial-run drop. Didn't I tell you why I was coming to town?" Samantha scrunched her eyebrows as she looked between Laney and me.

"You just said a convention. I assumed it was some psychology convention," I said.

The girls' mouths had fallen open. Skye recovered first. "Mom, can we go watch?"

Megan nodded her head vigorously in agreement.

Laney consulted the calendar on her phone before her face grew long. In a disappointed voice, she answered, "I'm sorry, girls. I've got some client meetings before I leave town that I can't skip—"

I interrupted, "I'll take them." Surprised that my mouth had engaged before I'd thought this out, I closed my lips before something else could leak out.

The thought of skydiving terrified me, but my girlfriend—that term still sounded weird in my head—had been encouraging me to stop being so anxious. Meghan would be impressed that I'd volunteered to go see this. I liked her and didn't want to screw up our new relationship by continuing to act too much like me.

Besides, tomorrow was supposed to be beautiful. It was late October already, and winter, with its overcast skies and rare rain during this time of drought, would start any time. I'd miss the nonstop sunny days of the other nine months of the year. I'd also finished preparing my presentation for Thursday morning, and otherwise, things at work had slowed down while we waited for the Sirius acquisition to go through.

"Really? To a skydiving thing?" Laney's eyes and mouth were wide open as she looked at me instead of Samantha.

"Yes, it will be fun," I said to convince myself as much as her. "Let's go get that ice cream." I stood up.

Megan cheered.

I screamed, as much out of fear as joy.

We all screamed. We were going for ice cream, after all.

Samantha held out her hand to me. I reached to shake it, but she laughed and slapped mine away. Apparently, I was supposed to know how to do her complicated hand gesture thingamabob without any prior training, practice, or instruction manual.

The girls snorted at my failure to give Samantha the proper celebratory hand greeting, and, in mere seconds, I'd reverted from cool back to normal.

As we got ready to leave, Skye decided to stay home to shower. I asked her if she was sick, but Laney waved me off. Twelve-year-old girls perplexed me. I mean, ice cream!

At the ice cream place, Megan and I climbed out of Laney's rental. We had taken hers, as I wasn't about to squeeze into the back of Samantha's sports car. A van next to us had a large "Zombie Response Team" sticker on the window and had its side door wide open. Even in the California suburbs, that was weird. Pointing the sticker out to Megan, I said, "They must have had an emergency situation to handle." I could be brave when it was full daylight and I was teasing my niece.

Although reasonably confident that I was mocking her, nonetheless, Megan gave a nervous laugh and darted quick glances all around her as we walked inside the shop.

We got our cones and walked outside to enjoy them in the warm, late October evening. By the time we got to our car, the spot next to it was empty, with half-melted cups of ice cream and napkins scattered on the ground.

Pointing to them, I leaned over to Megan and whispered, "Zombies must have won this time."

She screamed.

I chuckled, but Laney cast a glare on me that would have melted a zombie. She had just opened her mouth to chastise me when her phone rang.

"Yes?" She tried to put the other hand over her ear to hear

better in the tumult of the crowded ice cream parking lot but only managed to smear ice cream in her hair.

I grabbed her cone as she tried to listen.

"There's what? ... Now? At my house?" Her voice rose as she started to panic, and the crowd nearby quieted as her tension spread.

"Let's go. Right now," Laney yelled as she jumped into her car.

We raced back to encounter a fire truck, ambulance, and police car parked outside her house with their lights flashing. Laney's neighbor hovered on the porch near the front door. Inside, Skye sat on the couch, wrapped in a towel and looking mortified as firefighters tramped through the house checking for any danger.

Despite her foot in the boot, Laney practically flew to Skye's side and hugged her. Between Skye and the firefighters, the story came out. Skye had put Buddy in his crate before taking an extra-long shower, but she'd only closed the latch, forgetting to use the combination lock. Buddy should have been named Houdini. He'd escaped and somehow turned on the gas stovetop again. The new alarm did its job, calling the fire department. Skye had wrapped a towel around herself and run out of the house. The firefighters must have expected Buddy to cause trouble again and been cruising in the neighborhood because they showed up within a few minutes.

"This time wasn't as bad as the last one. Still could have had an explosion," said the same fire crew chief as last time. He must have kept close tabs on their frequent customers.

The shrill voice of Laney's neighbor came from the doorway. "Would the explosion destroy neighboring houses too?"

As everyone turned to stare at her, she fluttered her hands. "Should I call the police?"

Then, she noticed the cop standing next to her and began making little strangling noises.

To no one in particular, Laney muttered, "I'm going to make some calls."

I hugged the girls and got out of there with Samantha before Laney started blaming me for Buddy again. There was always tomorrow for that.

10

Wednesday

My conversation with the Santa Cruz County Sheriff's deputies didn't rank high on my list of most successful meetings. I did avoid arrest, though, which counted as a positive outcome in my book. The deputies didn't appreciate my suggestions, or my sense of humor. Sergeant Mace Jackson kept his feelings under wraps throughout the meeting, barely saying a word. Since the deputies didn't seem to like me, Mace probably wanted to keep them from learning how well he and I worked together.

Afterwards, on my way to pick up the girls from school, I called Raj to tell him about my meeting. "I got to see the inside of the police station and everything. It was cool."

"That is great." Raj's flat voice didn't match my level of excitement.

"Well, you missed a cool meeting. Did you have any more ideas about how Larry died?" We had—okay, I had—spent the morning in the office brainstorming ideas to bring to the police.

"I have been at work, unlike some people …"

Ouch. Normally laid back, Raj seemed high-strung today. In the background, I heard him typing. He was writing code while talking. There were plenty of days that I couldn't write code even in complete silence.

Raj continued, "Is that all? I have to complete this before I leave on holiday."

How could I have forgotten about his upcoming three-week vacation to visit his family in India? Without Raj, the office would be boring, even though I now had the monthly cake days in my calendar. We sang a lame "Happy Birthday" song and then everyone got free cake.

I tried again. "Well, take a break. Let's come up with more ideas for the investigation. The police are stuck. They're waiting for the autopsy results before they do anything else."

"I think the police will know what to do." The typing sounded louder as his voice faded.

I was losing him. "Come on, Raj, work with me here. Larry needs closure." On a whim, I threw him a curveball. "Do you think Sean Peters killed Larry?"

This grabbed his attention, and the typing stopped. "What? Why would he wish to do anything to Larry?" He paused before adding, "You should not upset Sirius' chief of staff. He could be our boss soon."

"Not if he's in prison for killing Larry!" I didn't like Sean. He was too young and too fit.

"Maybe your friend just died. No murder or anything suspicious. Sometimes people die for no particular reason. It is very sad."

It wasn't time to be sad. It was time for action. "Can you do a search online for Sean Peters and Larry? Maybe there's something weird about them."

There was a pause before Raj spoke again. "I see many articles about Sirius." After a longer pause, he said, "These biology terms are confusing. They are unfamiliar words to me."

An idea struck me as my Rover car neared the girls' school. "What about Gloria? Do you see her name in there?"

"Biology is not simple like engineering. Have you ever read some of these papers? If we will need to read such papers as part of Sirius, then perhaps we need to study biology."

I was still stuck on Gloria. "Maybe she's involved too. She could have been part of that secret project that Sean wouldn't tell us about. Maybe they were researching some dangerous biology project, like cloning humans."

"It is like another language. I am unable to read all these Latin words quickly. I will have to access a biology dictionary on the airplane to complete this translation."

I was on a roll. "But it all went wrong and the clone escaped from the secret lab in the middle of the night. Maybe Larry had to go chase him and got killed." My heart was racing now. This idea hung together. Movies were made with sillier plots.

Raj abandoned his confusion over biology vocabulary to focus on a more familiar form of illogical nonsense—me. "So now a clone killed him, not Sean?"

Raj's skepticism snapped me out of my crazy line of thought.

I answered Raj's question. "Okay, you're right. That could have been a movie I watched recently. But maybe Gloria is involved too."

Raj started typing again. "I do not see anything with all three names—"

"I've got it," I interrupted Raj. "Sorry." I'd been working on not interrupting people, but when I got excited it was hard to hold back. "I think Gloria and Larry were secretly dating. What if Sean was interested in Gloria too and he tried to break them up? Sean could have lured Larry into the woods, where they got into a fight, and then he accidentally killed Larry before trying to cover it up by stealing his EpiPen."

"Was this another movie you watched?" Raj asked in a dry voice. Sometimes he lacked sufficient imagination.

"No, I don't like romantic flicks," I said, dismissing Raj's skepticism. "This could be it. Gloria acted strangely on Monday when I asked her about Larry. Yesterday, Sean acted weird too." I snapped my fingers. "You know, her house isn't too far out of the way. I think I'll stop by and see if there's anything suspicious going on."

"I do not think that is wise." Raj always advised caution.

But caution was not getting us any closer to ending this investigation, although I realized Gloria was unlikely to be home in the middle of a work day. Plus, stopping by would make me even later to pick up my nieces for Samantha's skydiving practice. "Okay, I'll call Mace. He can investigate this angle while we're waiting for the autopsy results. He's probably bored sitting around anyway."

Raj tried to rein me in. "Perhaps you should leave the police alone. It is possible Larry died from a heart attack."

"No, that doesn't make as good a story. These sorts of things always get complicated." I knew because I'd watched lots of mystery shows. It was never the simple, obvious solution.

I hung up with Raj and was about to call Mace when my friend's words sank in. He was planning to spend his flight home to India studying biology terms to understand the documents he'd found in his internet search. What a great friend. I sent him a text to thank him for his help and told him not to worry about reading the scientific papers. Then, I called Mace.

"Now what?" he grumbled. "You know, I already drew the short straw once today."

I quickly outlined my love triangle murder scenario to him.

Mace cut me off before I could finish explaining the theory. "I'm only going to suffer through one crazy conversation per day and I reached my limit with you at the station."

He hung up.

My shoulders drooped in disappointment as the Rover car stopped at the school entrance. This wasn't the way partners should treat each other. Then I realized that the deputies were probably still in the room with Mace, so he had to act that way. He'd probably call me later to apologize. On the positive side, he basically gave me permission to call him once a day to discuss new theories.

Shaking off my momentary flash of distress, I got out of the Rover car in a happier mood and told the car to "stay."

That new "Stay" feature had become so popular Rover had to restrict customers from using it during busy times. I was proud to have helped turn Raj's idea into reality. Now that he was getting more attention as a great engineer, I also wanted to stand out by coming up with a successful new product feature all by myself.

I had an idea percolating. In fact, more than percolating. It was fully baked. I wasn't sure if I got the analogy right because I didn't drink coffee, but tomorrow was my big day. My boss had scheduled me to present a proposal to the Rover executive staff for approval. I was shocked that my boss admitted to liking an idea of mine.

Distracted by daydreams of tomorrow's big presentation, I pushed on the door to the school office and slammed right into it. I backed up, this time noticing the attached sign on the front that read "Pull." Hoping no one had noticed, I reached for the handle, pulled the door open, and walked inside.

"Mr. Golden, we would appreciate it if you would try not to break school property." As always, Mrs. Quarles, the school secretary, greeted me in her warm and pleasant fashion. She stood erect behind the counter, straightening the already neat stack of papers in front of her.

"Hello, Mrs. Quarles, nice to see you again too." I greeted her with a wave and a smile, which I hoped didn't look too much like a grimace.

She responded with a loud sniff.

"I need to pick up Skye and Megan early today to take them to see their cousin." I held my breath, hoping this would work. I had maintained a firm yet polite tone of voice, stated what I needed from her in a clear and concise manner, and plastered a smile on my face to boot. Just like that internet article had suggested for influencing others.

Mrs. Quarles harrumphed. Crossing her arms over her chest, she added, "School isn't over yet. It is important for the girls' education that they remain in school for the full instructional period." She picked up some papers from the counter, then turned her back to me and walked away.

Stymied, I didn't know what to do next. I'd tried my best and failed. The article hadn't covered what to do if the other person refused to listen to your reasonable request. I pulled out my phone and called Laney.

"I can't believe you. You can't even handle a simple situation." Laney sounded disgusted. "Put her on."

Easier said than done. It took me a minute to get Mrs. Quarles' attention, as she remained resolutely facing away from me. Eyeing me with disdain, she returned to the counter at the slowest possible pace. She took the phone from me and said, "Hello, Mrs. Tran. Is your foot doing better?" She managed to frown at me while maintaining a friendly phone voice. To Laney's response, she replied in a solicitous tone, "Good. I'm glad."

Pausing again while Laney spoke, she responded, "Oh. Well, why didn't he say so? Of course. Yes, yes. I'll take care of it right away. Okay then, take care." She started to hang up and then added, "Yes, I'm looking forward to seeing you at the PTA meeting tomorrow too."

Without glancing in my direction, Mrs. Quarles pulled an old-fashioned wired microphone on her desk close to her mouth, flicked a switch on the equally old-fashioned switchboard, and instructed Skye and Megan Tran to come to the school office right away. At least that was what I thought I heard over the howl of the microphone feedback.

After she ended her announcement, she slid my phone across the counter and turned the full force of her attention back to me. Pulling in her chin and lowering her brow, she shook her head in stern rebuke. "Why didn't you tell me the girls were going on an independent field study project today?"

I was impressed. Laney wasn't usually the sneaky one in our family. She must have been taking lessons from me.

*****

As the girls and I got out of the Rover car down south in Hollister, we craned our heads up to watch the skydivers drifting down into the fields around the small air field, stretching out the kinks from the ninety-minute ride while we took in the scene. Most parachutes were white, but different colors dotted the bright blue skies. The sounds of small planes taking off and landing echoed all around us. The surroundings were as pretty as a postcard, as long as I avoided thinking about the parachutes.

A small crowd had gathered on portable bleachers in a field to the side of the landing strip. In front of the bleachers were several targets on the ground. Skydivers drifted all around as they aimed for the targets. We headed in that direction too.

A small clump of skydivers clutching their wadded-up parachutes laughed and chattered with excitement as they walked past us. They wore a variety of helmets that looked little better than many bicycle helmets. How could something so flimsy keep people from smashing their heads in if their parachutes didn't work? Would they be thinking, "Oh, too bad my parachute failed, but at least I have this awesome helmet so I won't die when I hit the ground." There was a reason that scientists referred to the maximum speed of falling to earth as "terminal velocity."

Although the setting was beautiful, my anxiety billowed as the scene sank in. "Why?"

I must have spoken aloud, because Skye answered, "Because it's fun, Uncle Marty."

"Look at all the cool colors." Megan pointed up at all the people who were falling out of the sky. On purpose!

The whole thing made no sense. Flying in airplanes was scary enough, with all that rattling and bumping around, not to mention what felt like sudden, death-defying drops during storms. At least the planes had engines and some complicated magic that made their heavy bodies stay up in the air. Pilots trained thousands of hours to learn how to land safely and keep the planes from losing the magic mojo that kept them from dropping out of the sky.

"They're crazy," I mumbled.

"No, it's fun, Uncle Marty." Megan's singsong voice made it clear she thought I was being funny.

This wasn't funny. These crazy people jumped out of small planes, which were barely safe as it was. To make matters worse, these nuts thought a few flimsy yards of nylon were enough to save their lives. How could nylon protect someone from falling to their death? After all, I'd seen ads highlighting how nylon shirts dried faster than cotton because nylon LET THE AIR THROUGH.

As I watched a bright red parachute and one with a psychedelic sunburst drift to a landing right by the targets, I tried not to think about the thin little strings that attached the skydivers to that unreliable nylon. If I ever got dragged, crying and pleading, to skydive, I'd bring a whole roll of duct tape to attach myself to that parachute. Or maybe the plane.

"Uncle Marty! Come on. She's here," yelled Skye. She and Megan were a dozen yards in front of me, jumping around and waving like lunatics at the landing jumpers.

The skydiving spectacle must have scared me to a halt. Despite my reluctance, I pushed forward and joined the girls as Samantha and her friend gathered up their flimsy nylon parachutes.

"Woo-hoo! That was awesome!" Samantha was pumped as she gave her friend another high five. "Heya, Cuz. Meet my friend, Izzy. She organized this whole shindig." Samantha gestured to the shorter and younger woman next to her who wore yellow goggles with yellow clips on her rigging to match her psychedelic sunburst parachute.

"Nice to meet you," she said. "I hear from Samantha that you work at Rover, is that right?" She had a broad smile, as if she too had enjoyed her terrifying drop to the earth.

I nodded and shook her hand as she pulled off her helmet, revealing wavy brown hair.

"Well then, you should probably call me Isabella. I go by that at work, and I guess we'll be part of the same company soon enough."

I must have looked confused, because Isabella explained, "I'm the executive assistant for Doug Samerson at Sirius."

"Oh," I said, surprised to meet yet another person from Sirius. If this kept up, I'd know the names of more Sirius employees than Rover employees by the end of the week. I straightened up and made a mental note to behave myself. I tried to remember what that article had said about meeting coworkers in social situations.

"Don't get your knickers in a twist, Cuz." Samantha slapped my shoulder.

I must have displayed some marker of anxiety. *Gotta work on that for poker night.*

Samantha continued, "Izzy's cool. She organized all this in her spare time. Been down here all week setting everything up." Samantha pulled off her own helmet and vest, unveiling a Red Sox T-shirt.

As a longtime San Francisco Giants baseball fan, my scowl was automatic. "Well, that's not as bad as wearing a Dodgers shirt, but you shouldn't be wearing Red Sox gear here in Giants territory."

Samantha threw her head back and laughed. "I had to. I needed to match my chute. Not quite Red Sox red, but close enough." She pointed her chin at the red parachute gathered in her arms.

Megan and Skye asked a million questions as we strolled back to the parking lot. I hadn't met Izzy—Isabella—when I'd visited Sirius because she had taken the week off to manage this skydiving event. Like most executive admins that I'd met, she seemed smart and friendly, yet direct. She didn't hesitate to correct the girls' misunderstandings about parachuting while switching gears seamlessly whenever different skydiving event workers approached her with questions along the way.

"Can we get some popcorn?" asked Skye.

"Yeah! And Milk Duds," added Megan. To Isabella and Samantha, she explained, "You mix them with the popcorn and eat them together. That's how my mom showed us. It's best when the popcorn is hot, then the Milk Duds get kinda gooey."

"Never heard of that. Sounds awesome. Get some for me," said Samantha, reaching for her wallet.

"I'll try it too," said Isabella, slapping away Samantha's attempt to pay. "Tell the concession staff these are all for Izzy."

The girls yipped a thank-you and beelined to the concession stand.

Isabella watched the girls and then turned to me. "Maybe you can help me?" Her tone was more serious without the girls nearby. "Someone has been texting me these nasty pictures of a naked man. I know how to block a number on my phone. I do it every time, and then I get another gross picture from a different number." She frowned and looked over at Samantha. "I didn't want to say anything to people at work. It's hard enough getting respect from all the men, you know?"

Samantha nodded in agreement, her earlier ebullience fading. "Do you know who's been sexting you?"

"No. His face is never in there." She paused. "Just other parts. Mostly one in particular."

Samantha's face turned red as her anger grew. "Sicko. Well, we'll just have to solve this, won't we, Marty?"

Surprised that she'd committed me, I didn't answer right away. I knew of services that allowed people to get disposable phone numbers. Maybe whoever was sexting Isabella had used one of those services to mask their own number and make it easy to keep switching numbers with each text. I wasn't an expert on telecom networks, so I didn't have any idea how to stop them. I wasn't about to admit that in front of Samantha, though. She didn't look interested in hearing excuses.

"Um ... Sure. I'll look into it."

Samantha nodded and Isabella gave me an appreciative smile. Then, Isabella poked fun at something Samantha had done during the descent and they reverted to teasing each other.

After hearing about the guy who was harassing Isabella, I felt a little selfish for bringing up an unrelated request. Then, I figured agreeing to help the CEO's admin had to earn me a few credits, so I interrupted them. "I did have something else I wanted to ask Mr. Samerson, if there's a chance that you could bring it to his attention privately." Getting Samerson's answer without Peters around could make all the difference in figuring out what happened to Larry.

Isabella stopped in mid-tease and flipped into problem-solving mode. "Sure. Let me jot it down." She reached for something before coming up empty-handed and shrugging. "Sorry, I forgot I'm on vacation this week." She gave a wry laugh. "I feel naked without my notebook. Everything goes in there. All my action items, things I want to learn more about, even personal stuff." She laughed again. "Organizing this skydiving convention has thrown me for a loop. With all the volunteers working remotely on different projects at different times, we had to use an online task management system. Call me old-fashioned, but I think writing it down on paper keeps me better organized."

I nodded like this made sense to me. *Be nice to the CEO's admin.* But using paper made absolutely no sense at all. Not even a little. That was like rejecting sliced bread. People have used their phones to manage their calendars, take notes, and set reminders forever. Even my dad did this on his phone. Why would someone resort to using paper? Maybe Isabella wasn't as smart as I'd thought.

The girls returned with the popcorn and Milk Duds. As we munched, Samantha said, "Mmhmm whahoo ..." before waving me to wait while she paused to finish chewing her Milk Duds.

Laney had strange concepts of what foods went together. Last month her girls conned me into trying some bizarre food combinations that they promised me she ate. Now they were trying to trick me again. I didn't fall for it and contented myself with handfuls of plain popcorn, just the way Orville Redenbacher intended.

Samantha swallowed and asked her question again. "Are you coming to watch the competition tomorrow? I'm gonna whup Izzy like a lazy dog in the woman's division." Although Samantha had lived in Boston for years and worked to develop a Boston accent, every now and then she would come out with these Southern phrases. She learned them from spending time with her other grandmother in rural Oklahoma while growing up. The combination of a fake Boston accent and Southern expressions always struck me as odd.

Interrupting her conversation with another event worker, Izzy laughed and punched Samantha on the arm. "No way, José. I'm beating you again like I did the last two years."

Megan piped up, "Can we go tomorrow? This is way better than school."

I shuddered to think of how I'd get them past Guard Quarles. I doubted Laney's trick would work again.

Skye rescued me. "We can't. Tomorrow is Megan's Brownies meeting, and I have to take a math test." She almost sounded excited about the prospect as she skipped away from us.

While Megan ran after her to complain that skydiving was cooler than Girl Scouts, I considered returning tomorrow myself. With Laney's and my lack of sports skills, I had never seen a family member win a sporting event. If I worked this evening, I could complete a final prep run for tomorrow morning's presentation. I could leave right after the meeting and, with any luck from the traffic gods, make it here in time to watch Samantha. I'd survived today and even sort of enjoyed it. Plus, Meghan would think I was extra brave for facing my fears twice in a week. That had to count for something when she got home on Friday night. I swallowed and said, "Sure, I'll come watch."

Samantha said, "Cool, Cuz! You want to go out with us tonight? We're going barhopping. That's how we got to be friends. We met on the podium when Izzy took first place at an event in Hawaii and then went drinking with some cute surfer dudes as my consolation prize."

I turned them down. It was either go drinking tonight or watch them parachute tomorrow. Besides, I wanted to swing by Gloria's house and ask her a few questions about Larry.

This decision felt good. And if Samantha won, then I'd have seen a Golden win a sporting event. If Isabella won, I could earn some brownie points for being the first Sirius work colleague to congratulate her. No matter what, I was sure to be a winner.

What could go wrong?

11

Thursday Afternoon

The Rover car woke me up with a soft chime a few minutes before it arrived at the skydiving competition site. For new Rover members, sleeping while the car drove itself took some getting used to. Lots of time logged in Rover cars made taking a nap during a ride no problem for me. In fact, the wake-up alarm had been my idea after an embarrassing incident when I arrived still asleep at a trailhead for a hike and some young kids woke me by banging on the car window and laughing at my startled reaction.

While Samantha and Isabella went out last night, I'd stayed up late practicing my presentation for this morning's important meeting with Rover's executive staff. My boss had been so pleased that they'd said yes to our proposal that he told me to take the afternoon off. Good thing, as I had planned to tell him I needed to do some "remote testing" anyway. Now I could save that excuse for another time.

Still yawning as the Rover car pulled into the crowded parking lot, I was startled by the strobe lights of police cars and ambulances near the grandstand. I stepped out of the car and made my way to the entrance to see what was going on.

Samantha was in the middle of a chaotic scene, surrounded by cops and volunteers from the competition. Her head hung as she clutched her arms to her chest. She shook as if she might be crying. Her skydiving harness was still on but detached from her parachute. A police officer stood awkwardly near her as other officers milled around, giving directions to everyone as they tried to organize the bystanders.

I pushed through the crowd of gawking people to get to her. "Sam. Are you okay? What happened?"

"Oh, Marty!" She grabbed me in a tight hug. Now I knew something was terribly wrong. Samantha played red hands or gave wet willies; she was not a hugger. "It was horrible. Izzy ..." Her body shook as she took a shuddering breath. "She's dead."

I gasped. "What? Who?" Overwhelmed by the confusion around us and Samantha's emotions, I pulled back out of her grip to see if she was hurt. She was shaking but otherwise appeared undamaged, at least on the outside. Then her words made their way past my erratically firing brain circuits. "Oh no! Izzy?"

I couldn't believe it. Izzy had landed yesterday with no problems and joked around with the girls and Samantha. She'd even eaten Milk Duds and popcorn with the girls. "That's horrible. What happened?"

Her voice quivering, Samantha answered, "Her lines got tangled, or her chute ripped, or something. She just fell. Her safety chute didn't work right either. I've never seen anything like it." Samantha waved her arms in front of her face as if to ward off some bad juju. "I've got to get some air. Leave me alone for a while, okay?" She staggered away from me and the crowd, heading to the side of the parking lot.

I kept an eye on her but didn't interfere as the police moved the crowd farther away from the grandstand and organized them into lines before beginning interviews.

"Sir, could I get your name?" A Hollister police officer stood next to me with a notebook and pen in her hand.

Why did everyone still use paper? "I'm Marty. Marty Golden."

She wrote it down. "We're getting statements from everyone. Could you please describe what you saw and where you were during the incident?"

"Nothing. I got here after the police. All I saw were flashing lights in the parking lot."

She squinted at me. "Can anyone verify that?"

"What do you mean? Am I a suspect or something?" Before panic could take hold, I remembered I did have proof. "I took a Rover car here, so the records can prove I'm telling the truth." I prepared to explain Rover only to be surprised that she didn't ask.

Maybe Rover was gaining more traction than I thought.

I asked her, "Do you know how it happened yet? How she died?" My heart started racing as the thought of falling out of the sky struck me again. "Did something happen to her parachute? You know they're just made out of nylon, right? Did you check her strap thingies, you know, her yellow clips? Maybe a terrorist cut her lines?" When I noticed her reaction, I stopped blabbering and wiped my sweaty palms on my pants.

"It sounds like you knew her pretty well and have all sorts of ideas about her gear. What's your relationship to her?" The officer stared at me, her eyes narrowing as she flagged down another officer to join us.

I explained that Isabella was friends with my cousin and pointed at Samantha, who was leaning against the hood of her rental car.

Managing to keep my imagination in check while the officers questioned me further, I avoided increasing my odds of imprisonment. She raised her eyebrows as I explained that my knowledge of parachute gear and its potential risks for failure or sabotage was based solely on internet research done before I'd come out to watch Samantha. Being paranoid wasn't a crime, thankfully, so she eventually moved on to the next person with only a warning not to leave the grounds until the police gave the all-clear.

I'm free! I'm free as a bird now. I hadn't even needed to reveal my secret partnership with Mace to avoid a longer visit with the Hollister Police Department. I'd save that winning card in case a follow-up interrogation got even more intense. Before I got too distracted trying to remember the rest of the lyrics from that long-ago song, I walked toward Samantha.

*****

Over an hour later, most of the cars had left as the police sent people home. An older police officer made his way over to where Samantha and I stood on the outskirts of the nearly empty parking lot. "Do you mind if I ask you a few more questions before you leave? I understand you were close with Ms. Martinez—"

"What's happening with Izzy, with her body?" Samantha stumbled over her words as she struggled with the loss of her friend.

"Well, first we're investigating, of course. We've had some unusual responses so far." He looked me up and down before returning his attention to Samantha. "That's why I wanted to ask you some additional questions. You went up in the same plane and jumped before her, right?" The police officer managed to simultaneously convey a sense of soothing sympathy and a professional focus on finishing his job.

"My jump slot was four or five positions before Izzy's. The planes circle the target so everyone gets the same chance to win without having to worry about interference from other jumpers. I landed before …" She trailed off.

The officer got to his point. "Did you see anything unusual during the plane ride before you jumped?"

Crossing one arm over her stomach and putting the other fist to her lips, Samantha stayed silent as she replayed the events in her memory. The officer and I watched her eyes move back and forth like a tennis match as she followed each scene in her mind's eye. Right before I entered a hypnotic trance from watching her, Samantha answered, "No. It was the same as yesterday. Izzy and I were trash-talking each other. Mostly to stay loose, you know. Most of the others onboard knew Izzy too and joined in. She ran this event, so most everyone knew her."

"Yes, it seems that way." The officer gave an encouraging smile. "Did she have problems with any of the other skydivers or workers here?"

"You think someone did this to her?" Samantha frowned and narrowed her eyes angrily.

The police officer hurried to pacify her. "No, not necessarily. We want to conduct a careful investigation. By all reports, it sounds like it was a terribly unfortunate accident." He winced before adding, "Skydiving is pretty risky."

I found myself nodding in agreement before Samantha exploded, waving her arms as her eyes grew fiery. "It is not risky when you know what you're doing. She's done hundreds of jumps. She instructed new jumpers."

"Sorry. I didn't mean to imply—"

Samantha didn't even notice he'd spoken. Her voice faltered as she dropped her arms in exhaustion. "Her main parachute and the reserve failed." She paused, her face not yet frowning, but all the elements were gathering in case a frown was called upon.

"Yes, I heard." The police officer continued in his calm yet direct tone. "How about before the flight? Do you remember anything unusual?"

"No way that happens ..." Samantha was off in her own world. I recognized the signs, having traveled to my own planet on a regular basis.

The officer patiently tried again. "Did anything unusual happen before you went onboard?"

Samantha spoke as if to herself. "Her main chute was fine yesterday, and I know she repacked it herself because we did our chutes at the same time. And her reserve was recertified right before the competition."

The police officer cocked his head. "We heard that the lines of her main parachute got twisted. Doesn't that happen sometimes?"

Glaring at him and entirely unaware of his question, Samantha broke in, "You've gotta figure out what happened to Izzy."

"Well, I'm trying to," the officer retorted with a forced calm. "Can you tell me if anything unusual happened before you went up?"

Samantha refocused on him, looking as if she'd only now heard his question for the first time. "Well, it was a little hectic. The jumps were falling behind with more wind than expected affecting the drops. That happens sometimes."

"Was anyone hanging around Ms. Martinez's gear?"

"There were a ton of people milling around. Jumpers were piling up in the staging area. The staff moved in and asked all the later jumpers to take their gear away so the earlier jumpers could find our stuff faster and get into our planes."

"So, you didn't see anyone hovering around her gear?"

"No, not specifically. But with all the extra people, it took us a little while to find our gear. You know, like maybe someone moved it to make room." She stopped again, her frown appearing.

"What?" asked the police officer, noticing her reaction.

"Well, it wouldn't take more than a few minutes to screw with someone's gear. That's why the staging area is supposed to be secured. Ever since that guy in England almost killed his wife by fouling her chutes, competitions have become more security-conscious. A few minutes in the Porta Potty with a chute and you can snarl the main lines or cut some slinks."

"What's a slink?" I asked, the officer nodding in confused agreement.

Samantha looked startled that I'd interrupted, forgetting that I was still there. "Slink. Soft-link. It's string that holds the risers to the suspension lines." At our blank faces, she explained further, "They attach the harness to the lines of the parachute."

String? I felt a little faint. String was all that attached the canopy to the parachute? My earlier conclusion held—skydivers were crazy.

Samantha looked at the police officer. "Someone could use a pocket knife to cut the slinks. Slinks never fail. I know I saw her yellow clips on her harness in the plane." She paused to reconsider. "Well, I'm pretty sure I did. Let's look at her chute to see if the clips are all still attached. And we should also check her reserve chute to see if the slinks are undamaged." She lurched forward, but the police officer held up a hand.

"Hold on. I promise we'll follow up on this, but I can't let you near the evidence."

"Why not? I know what I'm doing. I can surely tell if a yellow clip or a slink is there or not." Samantha's voice rose with indignation.

"I'm sure you can. All the evidence will be examined by independent experts, who aren't a ..." He trailed off awkwardly.

"Suspect? Are you out of your mind? How can you think I'm a suspect?" Samantha's voice rose higher. "She was my friend. I ... I ..." She started sputtering.

I pulled her away before she did anything she'd regret. The officer gestured that we could leave. The Golden family had made quite the impression on the Hollister police today.

Even though the steam had stopped coming out of Samantha's ears, she was still agitated when we got into her car. "They better figure out who did this."

"Maybe it was an accident." I didn't add that I agreed with the officer that skydiving was crazy dangerous.

"Cuz, do you think I'm stupid?" Samantha snapped.

Her phone dinged from somewhere in the car, but she continued, "There's no way both chutes fail for an experienced skydiver unless someone messed with them."

"Never?"

"No!" she said in a strident voice. "We repacked our chutes in the packing tent together after yesterday's jump. Izzy was always careful. And we both used the same pro to pack our reserve chutes. You don't want anything to go wrong with that." Her eyebrows knitted together. "This can't have been an accident."

I considered her words as her phone dinged again. I had felt the same way about Larry, and everyone thought I was crazy at first too. "Okay, I believe you. Who do you think might have wanted to kill her?"

Samantha sighed. "Everyone liked her."

"I'll tell you, I'm not sure about working for Sirius. It seems like a dangerous place." I shuddered. "This is the second person from there who's died this week. Did she know my friend Larry?"

She shrugged. "Izzy never mentioned him, but it's not that big a company, right? So, she probably knew everyone."

"Anyone give her problems at work?"

"Nah. She liked working there." Samantha paused. "Well, all except for this young guy who thought he should run the place. Always saying bad things about her boss behind his back when he thought no one was around. She told me she'd called him on it last week and they got into an argument." Her voice thickened. "Do you think that's who did this?"

"Was his name Sean?"

"Maybe?" She shrugged again. "That could be it." She pounded the steering wheel. "Oh, I don't know, Marty." A tear formed in her eye.

A third ding. She wiped her eye. "Are you going to check your dang phone?"

"It's not mine." Reflexively, I patted my pocket. "I thought it was yours."

"Mine's right here." She pulled her phone from her pocket, then twisted around as she searched near her seat.

I checked around my seat as well, my hand landing on the smooth, metallic surface of a phone caught on the floor between my seat and the door. "Hey, here it is." Using my fingers as tweezers, I pulled it up.

She grabbed it from me. "That must be Izzy's phone. It must have fallen out when she got out of the car this morning." She tapped to open it.

Does no one secure their phone?

"Ew." She dropped the phone on her lap.

I picked it up to take a look. Someone … some man had sent her a picture of himself. More precisely, a close-up of a particular part of himself.

I flicked it away, trying not to touch even the part of the screen that had displayed the picture. I probably couldn't catch a communicable disease from the phone's display, but one could never be too careful. Another picture, from a different angle, appeared. I tossed the phone back to Samantha like a hot potato. "Yuck."

"This must be that sexter Izzy told us about." She tapped the screen to display the phone number. "Call him. Maybe he'll answer when it's not Izzy calling."

My first reaction was to say, "You call him." Given her current mood, though, I restrained myself and used my phone to call the number. No one answered. I waited a moment and tried again. After a few rings, a recording announced that the number was no longer in service.

"Not only is this guy gross, he's also insensitive. It … it just happened." Samantha choked up again.

The sexter couldn't have known Izzy had just plummeted to her death, but this wasn't the right moment to point that out to Samantha. I waited for her to regain control before commenting, "Yeah, an insensitive sexter. Who'd have ever expected that?"

Samantha gave a light snort. "Always with a joke." She sighed. "Okay. Thanks. Distracting me helps. Let's go home." She started the car and pulled out of the parking lot.

12

Friday Late Morning

By midmorning, I was hard at work in my home office on some follow-up items from yesterday's exec meeting at Rover. Izzy's tragic death had given me bad dreams about Larry. Between that and my excitement over the outcome from yesterday's meeting, I'd had a restless night and gotten out of bed earlier than normal.

In general, I tried to avoid becoming too insistent that everything remain in its proper spot. Too many engineers were labeled obsessive-compulsive, which I didn't care for. We engineers just … liked everything in the right place. So, despite the early start this morning, things were back on track as I worked in my home office and a guest slept in my guest room. I stretched and nodded to myself in satisfaction.

I'd thrown on a comfortable Hawaiian shirt, not one of those cheap polyester types that people only selected for spur-of-the-moment decisions to buy a wacky design aimed at impressing their friends at the next party. Nowadays, everyone seemed to have a crazy Hawaiian shirt merged with a sports team's logo or a bizarre hybrid animal. Amateurs. My shirts were all soft silk with the requisite palm tree, parrot, or pineapple. Professional.

The door to the guest room opened and Samantha stumbled out. Bleary-eyed, she stood leaning to one side as she regarded me in silence. Her hair looked like she'd fought with her pillow last night and lost. "Humph," was her only comment as she padded off to the bathroom. Laney was the only true morning person in our family.

A while later, an assertive, "Cuz" startled me from my work. Samantha looked more awake, although her face appeared blotchy from tears. "We need to do something about Izzy."

"Sure." I shifted into problem-solving mode. "Does she have any family? I saw an ad for a funeral home we can call—"

"No. I mean we need to *do* something." Her emphasis on "do" didn't sound like she intended to visit funeral homes today.

I shrugged and spread out my hands. "What do you want to do?"

"Cuz, I *thought* you were some bigwig advisor to the San Jose detectives, like Sherlock Holmes? Practically an independent investigator. Didn't you go on and on last month about your police award ceremony? I thought you were *empowered*?" Samantha's technique of emphasizing certain words stung. She uncrossed her arms and moved them to her hips. The slight coloring of my cheeks must have made her suspicious.

I couldn't meet her intense stare, because I had exaggerated my status with the police. "Independent investigator" might have been a slight embellishment of reality. And my award ceremony might have been more accurately described as a hearty handshake from Mace's captain. Mace had shaken my hand as well, if that counted. Although the handshake had felt truly momentous to me back then, it now seemed a bit lackluster under this morning's interrogation.

"So ... you want to go to the cops?" I hedged, not sure if I had deduced her wishes correctly.

Samantha stuck her tongue out and blew a raspberry to show her disgust. "Cuz, I'm from Boston. Only wusses go to the cops. If you want something done, you do it yourself. I want to find the scumbag who killed Izzy and ..." Her hands twisted an invisible someone's neck.

"Do you have any idea who did it?" My extensive detective training had helped me zoom in on the critical missing component of her plan.

"Pfft." Samantha gave a contemptuous roll of her eyes. "If I did, there'd be a real neck between these hands." Already, Samantha's short time with Skye had proven eye rolling to be infectious.

Pushing back on my keyboard tray, I took an extra-long moment to creak to my feet, trying to buy a few seconds to come up with an alternative plan. "You know, Izzy said she wrote everything down in that notebook of hers. Maybe we can go to her apartment and see if there's anything unusual in it." Plus, this would let me look for anything that Sean Peters might have told her about Larry. Nothing like killing two birds with one stone. I ignored the momentary flash of guilt at my own bad taste in idioms.

She latched onto my idea with alacrity. "That's brilliant."

I preened.

"But she said it's at her office, not her apartment. We'll get it from there." She turned, missing my mouth falling open. "I gotta get some coffee if I'm going to function. Show me where your coffee is. I couldn't find it yesterday." She was halfway to the kitchen before I could recover.

I had to tell her we couldn't waltz into Sirius Innovation's offices without an invitation. This wasn't like her psychology office, where each therapist met with their clients behind closed doors. Also, I feared that informing Samantha I didn't have any coffee because I didn't drink the stuff would yield an even harsher reaction.

I was right.

"No coffee?" Shock mingled with dismay in Samantha's voice. "What kind of human being are you? Are you sure we're related?"

"I like tea," I mumbled. Coffee had too many options and was too complicated to order. And it tasted, well, like coffee.

"Tea's fine for the Brits or for people who read cozy mysteries, but I need coffee if we're going on this recovery mission."

My explanation that our recovery mission wouldn't be the slam dunk she expected went over as poorly as I had anticipated.

She growled at me. "This isn't some *Mission Impossible* movie. You're the smart one in the family, can't you come up with a plan?" With her PhD and several other advanced degrees in the family, her flattery was a blatant attempt to manipulate me.

It worked. She had a doctorate in psychology, after all, while I had a bachelor's in engineering. Really, there was no comparison. Whether by teasing or provoking a response, she'd always been able to get me to do something I shouldn't have done.

This time, her movie reference inspired me. I looked out the window, trying to ignore the autumn leaves dropping in the light breeze, while I pondered how our strike team would penetrate Sirius' heavily guarded offices. In quick succession, I considered and discarded several possibilities, in large part because we didn't have a *Star Trek* transporter or a super-quiet spy helicopter and rappelling gear. Also, I was scared of heights, so that last idea was definitely out even if it had made an awesome movie. Although I had already figured out a simple way for us to get into the building, I still had fun brainstorming more ridiculous approaches and making Samantha believe this was hard work.

"Okay. I have an idea that might work." I double-checked to make sure it didn't involve any heights. With an impish smile, I decided to push my luck. "But I can't tell you more without compromising the mission's integrity. It's strictly on a need-to-know basis." If we were going to do this, at least I wanted to reenact some of my favorite heist/thriller movies.

"Okay." Samantha stuck her head in the refrigerator. "Got any chow?"

I rocked back in surprise. "You're … you're not even going to ask?"

"Nope." But a snort echoed from inside the refrigerator, ruining her attempt to ignore me.

Somewhat mollified, I headed back to my home office. "I need to finish a few follow-up things from yesterday's meeting first." I also had to prepare something crucial for today's mission. "Let's get an early lunch and head over."

*****

Samantha insisted on going to Starbucks for coffee, and since they also had some salads sitting in the refrigerator next to the cash register, we ate lunch there too, as she used some crazy excuse of saving time. But salad isn't lunch.

I didn't admit to her that arriving at Sirius during the lunch hour was a smart idea. With any luck, people would have left the area near Izzy's office to eat, and hopefully none of her neighbors ate at their desk. People who ate at their desks always seemed to bring their smelliest leftovers, burnt them in the microwave, and then stunk up the whole floor for the rest of the afternoon.

We were sitting at our table in Starbucks, finishing our so-called lunch, when a hand slapped me on the shoulder.

"John, dude! How's it hanging?" Brody, my friend, barista, and, most recently, kayaking partner stood beside our table with a broad smile on his tanned face. His orange-tipped hair still glistened from his morning surf, or maybe some hair product. His name tag had a smiley face drawn under his name that was a different color from the one he wore when I saw him last week. Paying attention to details was an occupational habit of a good engineer.

"Hey, Brody. We should go kayaking again soon. This time I want to try surfing the waves back to shore without tipping over."

He laughed and slapped me on the back again. "Sure, man. I'm busy this weekend, but maybe next weekend?" Gesturing to Samantha, he asked, "Introduce me to your date?"

"No, man. Not a date. This is my cousin, Samantha. Samantha, Brody." They shook hands.

"Nice to meetcha." He gave Samantha a broad smile. "Okay, dude, I've got to clock in and get to work. I need a new board. It's rad, man." His hands waved as he waxed his pretend board.

After Brody left, Samantha looked at me, "He calls you John, Cuz?"

"It's a long story. He knows my real name now." I flashed a thumbs-up sign to Samantha. "We're cool."

"*Dude*"—again with the emphasis—"he's waaay cooler than you. Seems nice, too."

Finished with our meal, we got up and I carried our things to the corner. Starbucks must have decided that their coffee menu wasn't confusing enough for us mere mortals so they added a garbage and recycling area with a large sign of instructions. I couldn't make heads or tails of them to determine what went into which container, so I tossed everything in the landfill container. If we needed directions on how to throw away trash, life had gotten too complicated.

Lunch accomplished, Samantha and I were now ready for showtime. Our mission was on. We'd received no recall order, so we were going in. I didn't have any face paint or 3D-printed latex masks to pull over our heads, turning us into undetectable duplicates of the Sirius CEO. That was unfortunate, because really, how cool would that have been?

That brainstorm spurred a more practical concern—I still needed a costume for Halloween tomorrow night. I'd put that on my list. I didn't have a list, but I'd start one just for this. Perhaps we could stop to look for something appropriate on our way back to my apartment. If I found a Doug Samerson mask, then I'd buy a few of those as well. For future missions, after Rover was part of Sirius.

"Are you there?" asked Samantha.

I'd zoned out again. I needed to work harder to avoid that. I nodded and we left Starbucks.

We took Samantha's convertible to the Sirius offices. To soothe my conscience, I justified it was in case we needed to make a quick getaway. If Rover and our competitors were successful, then far fewer people would own such cool cars. Perhaps my next idea should be to have Rover offer cool cars to members who paid a premium fee. I needed to add that winner to my nonexistent list.

We walked to the entrance in silence, dodging the lunchtime crowd. Before we reached the front door, Samantha said, "So, Cuz, seriously, what's the plan?"

Ha! She had cracked first.

Not even bothering to hide my smug smile, I pulled out my Sirius badge that I'd kept from my previous two visits. With my picture printed on the front, it was a near-perfect match for the normal employee badges. I held out the second badge, an imitation that I'd made for Samantha in my home office this morning. Using a similar tactic last month had worked well, so I anticipated success today too. I ignored the little mental tug trying to remind me I hadn't actually passed through security with that other fake badge. We'd have to wing that part and hope for the best. "A wing and a prayer," as the saying went.

I explained the simplicity of my plan. The best plans always were. Timing our approach with care, we were going to walk up to the non-functioning badge reader, wave our badges in the direction of the busy receptionist, and walk right through. We would head up to the CEO's fifth-floor office and look for Izzy's notebook on her desk. Then, with notebook in hand, we'd make our way out of the building without running into anyone who knew me.

Samantha stopped dead in her tracks. We were now twenty feet from Sirius' front door. "Seriously. What's our real plan?"

Questioning the leader's plan in the middle of execution was a recipe for disaster. Hadn't Samantha ever watched a heist movie? Our mission was on the verge of failure. I thrust the fake badge into her hands and said, "Come on, live a little." *Payback felt great.*

Despite her outward bravado and normally high cool factor, Samantha almost botched her spy role. She must have been out of practice in doing crazy stunts with her cousins. Or, since it concerned Izzy, this time mattered more to her than simple youthful hijinks.

When I greeted the security guard by the front door, Samantha almost had a heart attack. Rotating her head like a jittery mouse watching for an attacking owl, she almost ran over a woman pushing a baby stroller as we approached the badge reader. When the mother glared at her, Samantha almost bolted for the car before I grabbed her arm.

"Careful," I boomed. "We've got to get back in time for our meeting without stepping on any babies." As the receptionist looked up from the package delivery guy who was demanding her signature, she raised her eyebrow and gave me a puzzled look. I pointed my finger at the receptionist before turning it into a wave and big smile like we were old pals.

Confidence was the secret. Pushing Samantha ahead of me through the narrow entranceway, I nonchalantly held the gate for a woman leaving for lunch.

The insistent delivery driver slapped the counter, drawing the receptionist's attention back to him. We were through, thanks to UPS's tight driving schedule.

Phase 1 completed as planned. And without incident.

Samantha took a few deep breaths after we rounded the corner and waited for the elevator. "Boy howdy, Cuz, you were smooth. Weren't you nervous that you'd lose your job at Rover if they caught you?"

I swallowed as my throat went dry and my breathing grew shallow. That possibility hadn't crossed my mind. I had been showing off for my cousin. She hadn't double dog dared me or anything, but she had been making fun of me for being too cautious ever since she got to town.

Hiding my discomfort, I pushed the elevator button again. "In for a penny, in for a pound," as the saying went. Dang, so many good ones wasted without Raj around.

The fifth floor was quiet during lunch. Growing more nervous as I approached the CEO suite, I slowed our pace, scanning for anyone who might recognize me. There was no sign of Doug Samerson or Sean Peters. They'd probably gone for lunch together and were busy dreaming up more visionary ideas to dump on their unsuspecting employees.

I checked behind us for a tail. A small group of people filled the aisle, walking away from us to the elevators. We were clear. I pointed two fingers at my eyes before rotating them to point at Samantha's eyes. Then I gave the silent universal hand gestures for "stay right here and stand guard."

"What are you doing?" she asked.

I sighed at the waste of my fine fieldcraft. Samantha needed more training before our next mission. "Just stand here and let me know if anyone comes." I moved out of the corridor bordering Isabella's cubicle to search her desk for her notebook.

A tan Moleskine notebook sat right next to her keyboard. Flipping it open revealed Isabella's name and cell phone number inscribed in the inside cover. What outstanding detective work on my part. "All right," I said in exaltation.

Phase 2 of our mission completed.

Using all the detective wiles I'd picked up from watching TV, I found the last page with writing by flipping open to the ribbon bookmark.

A hand clasped me on the shoulder.

I gasped.

Samantha stood to my side, looking at the page. "Is that it?" she asked in a loud stage whisper.

"Geez." As I caught my breath, I made a mental note to institute an extensive "Spy 101" basic training curriculum starting tonight. "Yes. If you're not going to keep lookout, at least be quiet and help me look for clues around here."

"Shouldn't we take it with us and get out of here?" asked Samantha.

Her logic made sense, but I couldn't admit that to her so I pretended I had a plan. "That's not part of the plan. We'll take a quick look to see if there's anything in here. If there is, we'll bring it to the cops. Otherwise, we'll just leave it here."

Isabella's handwriting was hard to decipher, her words crammed together onto each small page. Nothing suspicious appeared on the last page. My brain struggled to parse her handwriting into words and interpret the acronyms and abbreviations into English. Isabella had kept busy with a ton of action items and notes to herself.

A nearby noise startled me.

Glancing around revealed nothing out of the ordinary. I also needed more spy training, particularly on how to remain calm during a mission. Now that we were behind enemy lines, my nerves were jittery.

Returning my attention to the notebook, I flipped back a page.

"What are we looking for?" Samantha asked.

"I'm not sure, but I hope we'll know it when we see it… Like that." I jabbed a finger against the page.

The line was short and cryptic: "Larry—see soon."

"I knew it," I said, triumphant. "There was a connection between Isabella and Larry."

"Why'd she want to see Larry?" Then Samantha teared up. "Do you think she was dating him? She never mentioned anything to me about him."

"I think …" Then, as the puzzle pieces clicked into place, my voice grew more confident. "I think you're right. They were dating. After all, Isabella told us she kept personal notes in here too."

"If she was dating him, why would she need a reminder to see him?" Samantha's voice rang with skepticism.

Her reasoning was sound and made me pause while I sorted through the possibilities, weighing and assigning probabilities like the finely-tuned detecting machine I'd become. Without all my police experience, Samantha had to have missed something important. The most likely option slotted into place in my mind. "I think I know who found out they were dating." I pulled back from the notebook, feeling smug that I had figured it out.

Samantha didn't seem to notice my satisfied glow. "Cuz! I swear I'm gonna—"

I interrupted before the threat was issued. "Okay, Sean Peters, their chief of staff, discovered that Isabella and Larry were dating. He was jealous because he liked Isabella too. He got into a fight with her and then killed Larry so he could have her to himself." Then, a stray thought intruded and my voice faltered. "Or, Gloria still liked Larry and she found out Isabella and Larry were dating. She went insane with rage and killed him." Regaining my confidence, I added, "Or both Sean and Gloria worked together to kill both of them." I swatted away any remaining doubts and added,

"In any case, this is proof that Isabella and Larry were in contact. I need to show this to Mace for our investigation right away."

My satisfied glow returned. Samantha shouldn't beat herself up over missing the connections. After all, she didn't have my expertise. "Put this in your purse," I said, thrusting the notebook at her. Remembering what I'd seen in Samerson's office, I decided we deserved a quick reward for completing our spy work undetected. "I want to show you something fast before we get out of here."

"Shouldn't we skedaddle now?"

Her Okie-influenced phrases were a little much sometimes. "Come on. This is worth it." I was already halfway through Samerson's office door by the last word. Samantha's curiosity outdueled her hesitation, so she shoved the notebook into her purse and followed only a few steps behind me. She'd always been the first cousin to join me when we snuck into the kitchen for forbidden pre-dinner snacks during family reunions at the lake house.

The golden glow emanating from the wide-open bathroom door beckoned us forward.

"Whoa!" exclaimed Samantha as she noticed the glow.

"I know. I caught a glimpse when I met the CEO earlier this week." I stepped to the doorway to get a better view. "This is way more impressive than I'd thought. Look. Even the toilet paper spindle is gold." I pointed to it as Samantha crowded in closer to get a good look.

"It can't be real gold, do you think?" she asked in amazement.

That's when we heard the voices in the hallway outside the office.

They didn't sound like Samerson or Peters, but I wasn't positive. There was only one reasonable option for our escape. The fifth floor was too high for a diving exit through the window. Besides, that would hurt.

I pulled Samantha the rest of the way inside the bathroom, closed the door behind us, and twisted the lock. I put a finger to my lips.

Samantha rolled her eyes but didn't add any further commentary.

We stood silently in the golden glow, hardly daring to breathe while we waited for whoever it was to go away.

No such luck.

An authoritative voice rang out, "Hello? You in there. You need to come out." The knob rattled as someone tried to open the door.

We were still safe.

If we stayed quiet, maybe they'd go away or forget that they'd seen us. We could wait them out and sneak out in the middle of the night. It worked for ostriches, didn't it?

A firm knock on the door ended that pipe dream. "Excuse me, but you need to get out of there right now." This voice sounded stern.

The first voice returned. "The police are on their way. Don't make us break down this door."

The jig was up. I unlocked the door to face the music. This mission was impossible.

13

Friday Afternoon

Reality struck me hard. My stomach felt queasy and my head throbbed. This mission had started as harmless fun, more showing off for my cousin than anything. Until we got caught. What had started as a lark could cost me my job once Sirius acquired Rover mere weeks from now.

The two security goons frog-marched Samantha and me out of the CEO's bathroom and down the hall into a conference room. The younger one strode with his chest thrust out, chin up, eyes looking forward. He kept a firm grip on my shirt collar. This wannabe police officer, or prison guard, enjoyed the attention as people returning from lunch stared at our peculiar procession. It was understandable. Security guards become invisible to office workers—seeing them do more than drink coffee or stand by an entrance alarmed people.

That was how we got caught. I'd forgotten about the security guard by the lobby door. He must have noticed us slide past the barrier without a proper badge. The flaw in the plan was mine from the beginning.

I felt even lower.

We sat there in silence, not looking at each other, both lost in our own thoughts for a few minutes while the wannabe cop went to the lobby to escort the police upstairs. Real cops. Through the glass conference room walls, people gathered to gossip and look at the spectacle.

The two police officers had only collected our identification when Doug Samerson burst through the conference room door. "What's going on? Someone broke into the building? Were they in my office? Were they going through my files?" The CEO wheezed as he pulled out a handkerchief to wipe his forehead.

I tried not to hyperventilate. As soon as Samerson noticed me, my future at Sirius was over. I looked down, hoping he would leave soon.

An officer handed back my driver's license and said, "We just started questioning them. And you are?" She didn't seem happy about the interruption.

Samerson puffed out his chest and strutted a few steps. "I'm the CEO. I run this place, and I demand you search them."

The officer's face tightened. "We can't search people without probable cause—"

Samerson spit out, "But they were in my office. It's probable they stole something." He exaggerated the enunciation of the words, as if trying to make sure a mere police officer could understand him. "I want to press charges."

Charges? I looked up in dismay. We hadn't stolen anything. Sure, they would yell at us and throw us out of the building. I was familiar with that routine. But this created a whole new concern for me.

Then I remembered Isabella's notebook, with her name on it, resting inside Samantha's purse. I glanced over at Samantha. Her eyes were wide and she'd turned pale. She hadn't forgotten about the notebook. I felt the blood rush out of my face. I hadn't even considered the possibility of jail.

The officer narrowed her eyes. "What do you think they took from your desk?" She didn't react to Samerson's tone, her voice remaining calm yet focused.

How many years of training were required to stay calm in a tense situation? I couldn't even talk to authority figures without feeling my blood pressure skyrocket. To heck with the voicemail lessons I'd been studying, I needed police training on remaining calm in a crisis.

And in normal life. That would be helpful too. Would the police open up their training to civilians? What about for those of us who were secret partners with a detective? If we weren't also in prison, that is.

"Oh, it's not on my desk ..." A bead of sweat formed on Samerson's forehead as he stopped himself and took a breath, his eyes racing from side to side. "I mean, there's something ... something top-secret." Gaining confidence, he added, "Yeah, they could have taken our top-secret business plans. From my desk."

The police officer's face didn't give anything away as she gave a half-hearted nod. "Okay. What do those look like?"

The wannabe cop jumped in. "They've got these hard red covers, and they're about this big." He held his hands a foot apart. Perhaps he hoped to get a recommendation to the police academy in return for his helpfulness.

The officer raised an eyebrow and turned toward us with her own exaggerated show of deliberateness. She looked at me, with nothing in my hands but clammy sweat, while I quickly glanced down again, trying to hide from Samerson. She then rotated to look at the small purse in Samantha's lap.

It was nowhere near large enough to hold a rigid folder. Izzy's small notebook was an entirely different story, however. I heard the officer's skeptical "Hmm."

Samerson's gulp was audible in the now-quiet room. "Maybe they took something else. I have a lot of sensitive papers." He swallowed again. "Very sensitive. They could have stuffed those in her purse."

Samantha clutched her purse to her stomach.

I snuck a surreptitious glance when the wannabe cop cleared his throat. He must have decided he was invited to participate in this conversation too. "No, they didn't—"

He stopped when he saw Samerson glaring at him.

Samerson didn't seem to appreciate the extra effort. The wannabe might need to apply to the police academy sooner than he had expected.

The wannabe lost his enthusiasm, but, still eager to show his professionalism to a potential colleague, he finished his report to the officer. "They paused outside your door for a little while before going into Mr. Samerson's office. They didn't have enough time in the office to touch anything. They must have hurried straight to the bathroom and shut the door."

"My bathroom?" Samerson's face twisted in disgust as he imagined what we might have done in there.

I didn't like whatever he must have been thinking, so I blurted out, "She's my cousin—" I broke off when Samerson recoiled again as he looked at me.

"Hey! You're that ... Aren't you that engineer? The one from Rover, right?" So busy trying to protect whatever secrets were hidden in his office, he hadn't registered my face until now.

I kicked myself. If I hadn't spoken, he might never have realized I was about to become a Sirius employee he could fire. With an unhappy frown, I gave him a curt nod. *Yes,* that *engineer. The not-so-bright one.*

As Samerson realized his security goons had tailed us closely and we hadn't taken anything from his office, his face formed an unpleasant facsimile of a smile. "Officer. He's basically an employee here, so there's no crime involved. We can handle things internally—as a personnel matter. There's no need to press charges." He attempted a more pleasant expression as he reached out to shake the officer's hand and dismiss her. He no longer needed her services.

The officer, however, didn't work for Doug Samerson. She took his hand, then pushed him out the door. "Thank you for your assistance. We'll let you get on with your very important meetings and finish up in here on our own."

Without saying a word, her partner maneuvered the two security guards out the door right behind Samerson, then leaned on the closed door to keep them out. Mace needed to take notes—this was how partners should work together.

The female officer turned back to Samantha and me, still sitting in our chairs. "So, what were you doing in his office?" Although her tone was still calm, the intensity had returned.

I settled on the truth and, almost, the whole truth. "I wanted to show my cousin the gold bathroom in Samerson's office." True, if incomplete.

"Gold bathroom?" The officer sounded confused. This was an office building, not some palace. Looking around this glass-walled conference room and the typical office hallway outside didn't alert one to the existence of a private gold bathroom.

Despite myself, I got excited. "Yes. It looks real. I mean, maybe it's just gold leaf, but still, that's crazy. Even the toilet is gold. And the toilet paper holder."

Before Samantha could speak, the officer leaned in closer to me. "You do realize this wasn't okay, don't you?" She looked hard at me, trying to discern whether I was certifiable or just an idiot.

I chose idiot and gulped. "Yes. I mean no. I mean I know it wasn't okay." I ran out of steam. To go any further would mean talking about Isabella and Larry and my theories about the conspiracy to kill them. Coming up with those theories was fun, but I didn't want to go to jail for them. Or the insane asylum. I admitted to stupid, not insane.

Samantha tried to help. "Officer, it was my fault. I've been teasing him since I got to town and he wanted to show me the gold bathroom ..." Then, she stopped too, clearly not sure where to go next.

"Well ..." The officer dragged out the word, trying to figure out what to do with us. It was evident she'd assessed our threat level and concluded we were harmless fools. On the other hand, the police had been called to handle a possible burglary, so she didn't seem willing to let us walk away with no consequences.

Before she could select an outcome we wouldn't like, I took a stab to see if I could help resolve this in our favor. "Officer, I've been consulting with Sergeant Mace Jackson on a case that may be related to Sirius."

She looked at her partner and smirked. "Is that so?" Her partner snorted from his post blockading the door.

No guts, no glory, right? Even though she didn't respond as I'd hoped, I doubled down on this approach. "Yes. We, uh, worked together to solve a murder last month." At least I managed to avoid using the "partner" term that Mace insisted I never use again.

"Well, let's just check out this little story, shall we?" She pulled out her cell phone and dialed a number.

From five feet away, I could hear Mace's response to her question clear as day. "He said *what?*" He must have lowered his voice after that, because I couldn't make out any more of their conversation.

Her smirk now turned into a bemused smile as she hung up with Mace and looked at us. "Sergeant Jackson has requested the pleasure of your presence. He wants us to bring you in." She jerked her head to the door. "Right now. Let's get going."

My worst fear was coming true. Jail.

She kept up the rear guard. She might not consider us dangerous, but she wasn't going to let us out of her sight.

Our unusual procession made its way down the hallway past all those staring eyes, crowded in for an awkward elevator ride, piled out into the lobby, then loaded into a black and white squad car. The officer wasn't interested in our request to follow them in Samantha's car, so we sat in their cruiser's uncomfortable plastic back seat.

Beside doors with no handles.

I was going to jail.

My phone buzzed—Meghan calling to chat before she flew home from her business trip. I hated not to answer, since we were in a new relationship and all, but I let it go to voicemail. I needed more time to come up with a good story to explain what had happened to us this afternoon. I'd see her tomorrow morning, and then at Laney's house, where we were supposed to help out with trick-or-treat duty. If I wasn't in jail.

*****

I spent the ride staring at the metal sheeting that shielded the officers' seats from their backseat "guests." We could barely see them through the super-thick shatterproof plastic separating the front from the back. The windows were barred and covered with wire mesh … a preview of my future living arrangements?

With my one call from the police station, who should it be? My kids were on the East Coast and still in college, so not my best options. Laney might decide to bail out Samantha and leave her brother in the clink overnight. That left Meghan, but she wouldn't land at SFO for hours. Brooding over my fate and poor options for rescue, I sat absorbed in my own world.

My phone's buzzing startled me. Raj had sent me a text. *Raj, my buddy!* Of course. Why hadn't I thought of dependable old Raj to bail me out? I started to tap out a response when the car pulled to a stop and the engine turned off.

My heart raced. I wasn't ready to face this. I took a deep breath and looked up to greet my destiny.

Starbucks.

Instead of the police station, we'd stopped at the same Starbucks where I always met Mace. Perhaps with all the cutbacks, he no longer had an office at the San Jose Police station? Maybe the Starbucks kitchen had a secret entrance to the county jail. Would Brody bring us our meals?

I stilled my overactive imagination as the officers opened the doors and escorted us inside to Mace's table in the corner. This was it. The next few minutes could determine whether I slept behind bars tonight or in my own comfortable bed. I hugged myself to keep my shaking from showing.

"Sergeant. Here they are," said the female officer, standing erect yet not quite saluting Mace.

He rubbed his chin as he examined Samantha and me. "Thank you. You can leave them with me. I'll take it from here." Mace dismissed the officers, who left without saying goodbye. He scowled at us, not speaking or moving for a few moments.

Brody bustled out of the kitchen, saw us, and gave us an enthusiastic welcome. "Hey there. Want your usual, John?"

Mace answered for me with a brusque shake of his head. Brody gave me a confused look but easily shifted his sunny smile to his next customer, calling out a greeting to him. Sure, he could smile, he wasn't on his way to the Big House. Through my fear, I felt a pang of disappointment that I wouldn't get my last triple venti half sweet non-fat extra-hot caramel macchiato. Even condemned men got to choose their last meal. Despite years of not drinking coffee in favor of tea, I'd developed a taste for this unusual brew after some confusion at the Starbucks pickup counter last month.

"Sit," Mace commanded. His gruff, angry tone resembled his typical rumble, but I knew the difference.

We sat.

Mace surprised me with his first question. "You still haven't told Brody your real name?"

I stammered, "I-I did—"

He interrupted, "Never mind. I don't want to hear it." Looking back and forth to both of us, he asked, "What on earth were you thinking?"

Well, I didn't think we'd get caught.

While I was busy not saying aloud what I was thinking, Samantha answered, "We wanted to see who killed Izzy."

Mace blurted out, "Killed? Who's Izzy?"

Despite my fear of what lay in front of us, I jumped in. "Isabella worked at Sirius Innovation. She was the executive assistant to the CEO." I clenched my fists. "That's the same place where Larry worked."

"I'm sure a lot of people work there." He squinted at me. "You're not the police. You've got to stop this."

"But look at this—her notebook shows she knew Larry." Samantha pulled out Isabella's notebook from her purse and showed it to Mace.

He didn't look at it. Instead, he stared at Samantha. His voice grew dangerously quiet. "Where'd you get that?"

She pulled it back. In a quiet voice of her own, she admitted, "From Izzy's office."

His eyes never leaving hers, he shook his head again. With clipped precision, as if explaining to a child, he said, "You are not the police. You cannot sneak into places and search them. Or steal things. These pretend investigations have to stop. Or we'll have to stop you more permanently. Now, what were you doing there?"

My chest froze. Was he threatening us?

Mace spoke into the silence. "We could move this to the precinct, if you'd prefer."

I took a shuddering breath as I realized his definition of "permanently stopping" us had meant jail, not death.

The oxygen coursing back through my blood gave me courage. He had to listen to me. We'd solved that case together last month. In fact, I'd come up with my brilliant plan right here in this Starbucks. It hadn't gone quite to plan, yet it wound up working in the end. And all's well that ends well. "Look, first Larry's death is suspicious, and then so is Isabella's. Larry was working on a project with the chief of staff, and his office is right next to Isabella's cube. And she wrote in her notebook that she planned to see Larry soon."

Mace's forehead crinkled in concentration.

I was convincing him. He was listening.

"Give me that notebook."

I had done it. We were partners again. Now Mace could bring the awesome power of the San Jose Police down on Sirius Innovation and bring the villains to justice.

Samantha slid the notebook across the table, not wanting her hands to get too close to Mace in case he decided to use his handcuffs.

Mace picked up the notebook and, without opening it, dropped it into his backpack by the side of his chair.

I hadn't done it.

"But?" I said, shocked. "Aren't you going to help investigate? I think Sean Peters—he's the chief of staff—is guilty. He was working on a secret project with Larry, and he sits right next to Isabella. He probably got jealous that Izzy liked Larry and so he killed them." I hesitated as Mace's expression turned incredulous. I rushed to finish before he interrupted. "And Gloria. She works at Sirius too.

She was also part of the secret project and she used to date Larry. I think. She could have killed him because he got interested in Isabella. Or maybe they each killed one of them. I don't know for sure, but we've got to do something. You should question them." I pounded my fists on the table, almost knocking over his coffee.

"Do you even hear yourself speak? You're nuts. This isn't some make-believe mystery story. Everything isn't a conspiracy. You've got to cut it out or you will spend some time in jail."

I sat back, frustrated, until his words penetrated and I realized he wasn't taking me to jail. Well, at least I wouldn't need to beg someone to come bail me out today. Besides Raj, the others might leave me there after they heard why I was locked up.

"Can't you do something about Izzy?" Samantha's quiet voice interrupted Mace's scowl.

"She's the one who died in the parachute accident?" asked Mace, his voice now closer to its normal low rumble.

Samantha burst out, "It wasn't an accident. She was an instructor. She had hundreds of jumps under her belt. No way she messed up packing her chute and had a problem with her backup on the same jump."

"Okay. I don't know, but it's not our case. The accident ..." Seeing her face darken, Mace altered, "...her death took place down in Hollister, right?"

"They're only a tiny town. The whole department was there for the event. What if ..." Samantha paused as she considered her words. "What if the killer is from San Jose? Wouldn't you, shouldn't you, help catch him or her?" She sat back, looking hopeful.

Mace scrunched up his face, clearly not excited about getting involved. After a moment, he sighed in surrender, his commitment to helping people outweighing his displeasure. "Look, I'll call down there and see if there's any reason to believe it wasn't an accident and find out if they have a suspect from San Jose. But you can't be involved with his craziness." He waved a dismissive hand in my general direction.

I resented the implication. Samantha was every bit as crazy as me. She was family. It was a genetic thing.

She accepted her little victory. "Okay, thank you for helping." With her voice cracking from emotion, she cleared her throat and added, "This was no accident. Izzy was too good for that."

After that, there was nothing else to say. Grateful we were set free with only a lecture, I stood up to leave. It was time to get out while the getting was as good as it was going to get. After all, I fought the law and the law won.

Brody lingered by the door, taking far longer than necessary to straighten the posters hanging on a bulletin board so he'd be there when we left. "Hey, dude, everything okay?" he whispered out of the corner of his mouth so Mace couldn't see us talking.

"Yeah," I sighed. "Thanks for asking." I glanced back to see Mace already preoccupied with more paperwork. I pulled up my Rover app to order us a car. The police officers had dumped us with Mace, and I didn't want to press my luck by asking him for a lift back to Samantha's rental car.

Brody moved a flyer so it wouldn't overlap with a larger, colorful one advertising this weekend's Half Moon Bay Art and Pumpkin Festival. When I was growing up, this festival took place in early October. With California's long-term drought, lots of things had changed. Besides more wildfires and needing to take short showers so I didn't use up my water allowance, pumpkins took longer to grow. As a result, the festival had moved to the end of October.

Brody followed my glance. "You going?"

I scoffed. "Sit in traffic for over an hour each way across the mountains so I can walk around an overcrowded street and look at crap artwork? I don't think so."

Brody held his arms out wide. "Dude. Don't be a Debbie Downer. It's ginormous pumpkins, a Halloween costume contest, and alcohol. What's not to like? Besides, if it's too gnarly, I'll just catch some wave action."

I shook my head in disgust. All those crowds and traffic? "Not interested." I could stop at the local pumpkin patch if I wanted to look at a bunch of pumpkins. I added, "Besides, I'm supposed to be at Laney's by 5:00 p.m. to help with trick-or-treating."

"Sounds radical," Samantha chimed in. Her exaggerated California surfer accent cracked me up. Even Brody laughed.

With my kids grown, I missed trick-or-treating. I didn't like to admit it, but after all these years, I was looking forward to going with my nieces. Meghan had wanted to come too. With no kids of her own or young relatives nearby, she said it gave her the perfect excuse to enjoy Halloween like a child again. It was no surprise we were getting along well.

I still needed to pick up a costume before going to Laney's house, but I wasn't in the mood after today's fiasco. Perhaps Meghan and I could stop somewhere after we had brunch in the morning.

My Rover app signaled me. "Oh, it's here." Turning to Samantha, I said, "Let's go."

Brody gave us both fist bumps as we left.

As Samantha and I got into the Rover car, she looked at me. "*Cuz*. You and that cop. That was impressive." She raised her eyebrows. "Are you always this crazy or just when I'm around?"

14

Saturday Morning

When I stumbled half-awake out of my room in the morning, the door to Samantha's room was open. On the kitchen table, I found a note saying that she'd left early to drive up to Napa to toast Izzy and would be back later this afternoon. After our debacle yesterday, she'd given up on doing any more private investigations. As for me, since Meghan had been gone all week on her business trip, I wasn't disappointed that Samantha had taken off. Meghan and I didn't have anything planned yet besides meeting here to hit a brunch place nearby.

After showering, I waited for Meghan outside the apartment building. The weather was still warm in late October, so I didn't need a jacket to go with jeans and my new Hawaiian shirt. Meghan didn't seem to be a big fan of my other Hawaiian shirts, so I figured a new one would win her over. She loved Renaissance Faires, so I ordered a Hawaiian shirt online that had more of a Robin Hood theme with green, yellow, and brown leaves intertwined with bows, and arrows sticking out of pineapples. Hawaiian shirts had to have a pineapple or a palm tree. After all, I didn't want to be uncouth.

Meghan parked near me and got out of the car, walking toward me with a smile and a shake of her head.

I was happy to see her too.

I held her for an extra moment as we kissed before we broke apart. "Really?" She sounded incredulous. "That's what you wear after you haven't seen me all week?"

I pouted. "I got it for you. It's got a Renaissance Faire motif with the arrows and all the leaves and stuff." I waved my hand across the pattern.

She leaned in and pecked me on the cheek. "That's sweet … I think."

Pout over. "Let's go eat." I was starved. "That place fills up quickly. Afterwards, I was thinking maybe we could go to the Stanford football game?"

She hesitated, giving me a very sweet smile. "I have an idea. How about if we go somewhere else instead of that brunch place today?"

I was game, as long as food was involved. It was hard to resist her smile. Kickoff wasn't until 1:00 p.m., so we had time for another place.

"In the airline magazine, I saw an ad for something that looked fun," she said, leading the way to her car. "Let's go to the Half Moon Bay Art and Pumpkin Festival." Noticing my reaction, she stepped back to where I had stopped in my tracks and added a kiss on my other cheek. "Oh, come on, it will be fun."

Traffic, crowds, street food—all things I didn't enjoy. Sure, I put up with them if there was a sporting event involved, but not for a silly art festival. I steeled myself to tell her this was not going to happen. I looked her in the eyes, took a deep breath, and, with a calm voice, said, "Okay." My dad didn't raise no fool. This was a new relationship, and we hadn't seen each other all week.

She clapped twice in excitement. "Good. I was afraid you were going to say no."

No was an option?

*****

The drive was as long and painful as I had imagined. The search for parking was even worse. We finally lucked into a parking spot when a man wearing a San Jose Sharks hat with a cigar in his mouth jumped into a pink cheetah-print Mini Cooper and accelerated away from the curb right in front of us. Meghan giggled at the image. Hopefully she wouldn't share that visual with Laney as a suggestion for her new car's paint job. Ridiculous. Although, I did approve of the guy's hat.

We pushed our way through the crowds. The festival was every bit as annoying as I'd expected and without the reward of a football or baseball game to follow. I felt another pout coming on. Then Meghan grabbed my hand and I relaxed as I took in the beautiful, warm day. To quote a certain barista friend of mine, it was "chill." Hand in hand, we wandered back and forth past enough rows of artist booths to last me a lifetime.

The smell of the nearby ocean mingled with fried food and sunscreen. All that sniffing made me even hungrier. One big positive of coming here—funnel cakes. The brunch place didn't have those bad boys on the menu. After winding our way to the food area, we split up to get through the lines faster. I bought us some sausage links, and for some inexplicable reason, the funnel cake line was empty. I got my pick of the lot before snagging a table while Meghan stood in a long line for our drinks and a taste of some pumpkin smoothie concoction.

While I waited, I took a bite of my sausage. Just one. It wouldn't be polite to finish my meal before Meghan showed up with our drinks. A little quality control was acceptable, however.

"Why are you so cute?" came a woman's playful voice from my left.

I shifted on the bench and prepared to answer her. A young woman was crouched in front of her baby stroller, cooing at her baby. I closed my mouth, glad that I hadn't blurted out that if she thought my left profile was cute, she should check out my right side.

Meghan walked up holding her smoothie and two glasses of wine on a tray and sat down next to me.

"Oh. They didn't have beer?" Then, before she could answer, I corrected myself. "Thanks."

My appreciation must not have sounded too sincere, as Meghan's face tightened a little. She handed over a wine glass without saying a word.

The band started playing, so I didn't have to speak for a while as we ate and listened. Putting the sausage in my mouth sure tasted better than my foot.

After a few minutes, I felt someone staring at me but noticed no one nearby looking at me. I've never understood how you could feel a stare. Was that some remnant of powers from long-ago human evolution that had faded? What other superpowers had we lost? Were we ever able to fly? I got excited about this possibility and almost mentioned it to Meghan until I felt the stare again.

Wary, I glanced to the side. A person painted all in gold was staring at me while he stood like a statue outside a store named Southern Treasures. I stared back, careful not to blink. Performers like him entertain the crowds by freezing long enough for a new fool to walk by before scaring them with a sudden movement. I was not going to be that fool. Not today, at least.

I couldn't hold it any longer. I blinked. This guy was good. He hadn't moved or blinked in over a minute, unless he timed his blink for right when I did.

"Why are you staring at that mannequin?" Meghan leaned over me to get a better look.

Startled, I double-checked that she was looking at the same thing. "Are you sure that's a mannequin? It looks like a real person painted in gold."

Meghan scoffed. "It's missing ears." She stood up, brushing off any crumbs, and tossed her trash into a nearby container. "Anyway, it looks like a cool store. I want to go in."

I kept the groan to myself, although the whine leaked out on its own. "It's an antique store. Aren't we here to see the art?" Even the art booths would be more interesting than that. Everything in an antique store was old.

I followed Meghan into the store, careful to give the mannequin a wide berth in case she was wrong. The mannequin's creepy-looking, almost human eyes and realistic body painted all in gold would give me nightmares. Was Samerson's gold bathroom just a good paint job too, or did it really have any gold? What was he hiding in his office that he was worried Samantha and I had found?

Still pondering these points, I stepped into the store. Being away from the noisy street was a relief, of sorts. An older man wearing a cowboy hat over long, ponytailed white hair, tight jeans, and cowboy boots approached us. "Howdy and welcome to Southern Treasures." He whipped off his hat and bowed slightly to Meghan. "Can I get you some coffee while you browse?" He winked at her. "I add a little extra Southern Comfort to it to make you feel right at home. In fact, that's what I was going to name this place before my lawyer gave me some nonsense about trademarks." He never glanced in my direction as he took Meghan by the elbow and guided her deeper into the store.

Meghan looked from side to side at all the crap. "Oh, you have such lovely antiques here." She patted him on the arm, and he beamed in response.

"Well, ma'am, I tell people it's my Cowboy 401k plan. I collected all these beauties over the years. Once I retired and moved here, I opened up this place. Now I sell a little here, a little there, and I get by."

Meghan stopped in front of a small wooden stool with carvings in the legs. "Oh, this is adorable. Would you take $100 for it?"

The owner held his hat in both hands as he glanced sheepishly at the floor. "Well, you know I surely did fell off that truck. But it weren't yesterday. It would be downright criminal to let it go for less than $200."

They both laughed. I cringed.

They continued wandering and talking. I had to admit the owner had good taste, at least in women. He seemed to enjoy haggling with Meghan while he ignored me and gave scarce attention to the other patrons in his store.

We circled back to the small stool.

Meghan twinkled her eyes at the old man. "It would stroke my ego if you'd let this go for $145."

He nodded. "Well, honey, let's not stroke it quite so much and do $175."

She bought it for $150. Meghan wasn't a pushover, even when flirting.

As they haggled over what Meghan told me was "one last item," she said to the owner, "You know, if you keep charming me like this, we might end up married before we're done."

The old man slapped his knee like this was the funniest thing he'd heard in years. "I don't know, hun, you spend too much money. I don't think I can afford you."

They laughed together again, but I noted that he hadn't turned her down.

My phone rang. Neither noticed as I excused myself to take the call outside. Although it was noisier outside with a band at the corner, the call gave me a perfect excuse to escape.

Raj had granted me a temporary reprieve from more faux

cowboy nonsense. "Hi, Marty. When will you make it into the office today for the special project?"

Today was Saturday and we didn't have any urgent releases coming up. What was he talking about? "What special project?"

"Oh." He hesitated. "I assumed the boss called you too because Larry was your friend."

"Larry was my friend but the boss didn't call me. What are you talking about?"

"Sorry, sorry. The Santa Cruz Sheriff's Office asked Rover to do a search of our records to see if Lawrence Cohen used our service. The deputy said it is important, it is part of their murder investigation. I will go to the office in an hour or so."

Why didn't my boss ask me? In fact, why didn't the deputies ask me? I was part of this investigation, practically on the team. Larry was my friend. My longtime friend. I'd been at the campground, discovered his body, annoyed the sheriff's deputies, and then spoken to them more politely while Mace sat next to me. I'd discovered the connections to Gloria and Sean Peters. My annoyance grew. It was time to call Mace and get to the bottom of this.

"Marty? You there?" Raj asked, interrupting my internal fuming.

"Yes, sorry. I'm here. And, yes, thanks, I definitely will help. I'll call you right back."

I hung up and frowned at the mannequin. He frowned back. I swear he did. While I paced in front of the store, I called Mace.

He answered after a few rings. It was hard to hear him with all the music playing in the background.

"Mace ... Sergeant Jackson?" I shouted as I cupped my hand over my ear.

Wait. The same music was coming from the phone.

"Are you here in Half Moon Bay, too?" I yelled into the phone.

"Umm," was all I could make out from him.

He was here. I heard the same announcement in stereo, from the loudspeakers and via the phone's speaker. "Where are you? I need to talk to you right now about this search warrant for Rover."

Mace told me to meet him by the side of the stage. I promised to be there as soon as I grabbed Meghan.

I burst back into Southern Treasures, almost flinging the door open against the wall. "Hey, Meghan, we gotta go. I've got to talk to Mace. He's here, at the festival."

She was standing at the counter with the owner.

"Now, son, don't pitch no hissy fit. We're fixin' to finish up right soon." The owner didn't increase his pace or seem at all concerned about my urgent issue.

What was that saying about how your emergency wasn't my crisis? I watched the embodiment of that saying as he fiddled with his credit card machine. I reached over to help him.

He pulled it farther away from me. "Okay, okay, hold your horses. This here machine ain't no faster than a one-legged man in a butt-kicking competition. It'll finish when it finishes."

Meghan asked, "Mace called you?"

I didn't appreciate the incredulity in her voice. He called me sometimes. Once before this. This time, I was going to help out on a search warrant. We were going to figure out who killed Larry, together. I didn't want to talk about the details in front of the store owner. *Civilian.*

Before my head exploded from anticipation, the owner finished the transaction and handed Meghan her receipt. We walked out of the store, me carrying the stool and Meghan holding her other smaller purchases.

I started to explain what had happened when an attractive, well-endowed woman wearing a belly dancer outfit walked by right in front of me. If her clothing, consisting of not much more than a bikini, wasn't distracting enough, she was carrying a long horizontal pole that created the stoop for two large, colorful birds. They were attached to the pole via a chain through their beaks. Meghan stumbled into me as I slammed to a halt and waited for the spectacle to pass.

Meghan recovered from her stumble, noticed the scene in front of us, and demanded, "What are you gawking at?"

"Her toucans."

"Sure you are."

I didn't notice the dangerous note in her voice as something else caught my eye. "Do you see the EpiPen pouch on her hip?"

"So, which is it? Her hips or her 'toucans?'" She gave a disgusted snort. "Men." She walked off, away from the music.

How was it my fault that such a spectacle walked right in front of me? There had to be a joke starting with "two toucans walked by with a belly dancer." More important was her EpiPen pouch. Had the police found any fingerprints or other evidence on Larry's bag in his car? Was his EpiPen in there? Why had it been in Larry's car instead of with him? If a bikini-clad belly dancer could walk around with an EpiPen on her hip, there was no way he'd go out on a hike without his.

I hurried to catch up to Meghan before I lost sight of her. "I'm sorry. I almost ran into that woman and then she had those two …" Seeing the expression on her face, I adjusted mid-sentence. "… birds. Were they parrots or toucans?" I spoke faster as I noticed her frown hadn't disappeared and her pace hadn't slowed. "They were really beautiful. I hardly even noticed the woman. And her EpiPen made me think of Larry. Besides, I don't find her anywhere near as attractive as present company." I held my breath.

Meghan finally slowed her pace, looking over at me and taking pity on my befuddlement. After narrowing her eyes briefly to send home her point, she relaxed and actually chuckled. "Yeah, those birds were pretty. She really was too much, wasn't she?"

I let out my breath. "Yes, she was way too much." Agreeing

was the wisest course. Besides, who found so much coconut oil attractive?

Meghan asked, "What did Mace want?"

Mace! I'd forgotten he was waiting for me by the music stage. I turned us around and we made our way there as quickly as we could.

Mace's displeasure was visible from a distance. He sat on a chair at the back edge of the crowd with his arms crossed against his chest. Why was he here?

He glared at me as we approached. "That was 'right away?' You know, I have a life too."

His normal life disguise disappointed me. Most superheroes looked quite different out of their costumes, but Mace's civilian clothes looked much like his police uniform—tight-fitting, dark, and sharp-looking. I'd have to help Mace develop a better disguise; perhaps Hawaiian shirts would hide him in plain sight as well as keep him looking stylish. Like me.

Mace didn't care about my disappointment. "I don't want to be standing around waiting to talk to crazy people. I have to do that when I'm working."

Meghan sat down in the last empty seat next to him, her arms full with her packages. "Hi, Sergeant Jackson, how are you?" Her slight emphasis on his title and the extra twinkle in her eyes highlighted that she hadn't forgotten meeting him last month.

Mace's frown was overtaken by embarrassment sweeping over his face as he remembered their first meeting as well. He tried to remain professional. "Fine, thank you. How have you been?"

I jumped in before anything could go sideways. "I'm sorry. The store owner was flirting with Meghan and then—"

She interrupted, "We weren't flirting. We were negotiating."

"Then, a belly dancer walked by with these two beautiful—"

"What do you want?" asked Mace. He'd lost patience with both of us.

I swallowed the rest of my explanation and got to the point. "Did you know there was a search warrant served to Rover? I have to go look for any use by Larry? Why didn't you tell me?"

"First, I am not your messenger service. Second, I only heard myself a little while ago. Santa Cruz filed the request and they notified the different companies directly." His eyes flickered over my shoulder and back, but his face remained impassive. "Look, if that's it, then you better get going." He stood to walk away.

"Wait." I was confused. While his dismissal of me wasn't unusual, it typically took me doing something irritating before he ended our conversations. "What about Larry's EpiPen? Was it in his pack? Were there any fingerprints on it?" Then a possible reason behind the search warrant dawned on me. "Do the deputies think he took a self-driving car and met someone at the park?"

"I don't know. I'm only the liaison officer. I'll let you know if anything turns up." Mace hurried his response, clearly eager to be away from me.

"Dude! You're here. Totally righteous stool." Brody clapped me on the back, pulled the stool out from my arm, and sat on it, running his hands across the carvings on its legs.

After our discussion at Starbucks, Brody's presence here in Half Moon Bay didn't totally shock me, but I was surprised to run into him right after seeing Mace. After all, thousands of people were milling around this crowded mecca of pumpkin unpleasantness.

Brody's eyes and smile widened as he noticed Meghan. "Cowabunga! You and him?" He gestured back and forth between the two of us before stretching forward to hug her when she nodded. He didn't have to look so surprised.

Brody handed the water bottle to Mace while keeping the beer for himself. "Dude. It's Kona Longboard. Still sure you don't want some?" He offered Mace some of his beer.

"No thanks." Mace looked at Brody and smiled. At least that's how I interpreted the unusual expression on his face. "I'm on duty this evening."

I looked back and forth between them. "You and him?" I asked Brody, mirroring his tone and hand gesture.

"You got a problem?" Mace's rumble prevented Brody from responding out loud. Brody's broad smile and hand caressing Mace's shoulder answered anyway.

"No. I just ..." My voice trailed off. I've heard that opposites attracted, but this blew my gaskets. "I'm surprised is all." Minor understatement of the year.

"Okay, well, now you know." Mace shifted back into policeman mode. "Unless you have something useful to say, we'll be on our way."

I had nothing.

After they walked away, I picked up the stool, and Meghan and I headed back to her car. Still stunned by the revelation, I asked, "Did you know?"

Meghan's eyes sparkled. "Of course. It was obvious. Didn't you notice how they acted around each other at that Starbucks? You went kayaking with Brody, right? I'm surprised he didn't mention it."

How long had this been going on? I'd have to ask Brody. I glanced sideways at Meghan. Opposites attract? She was good-looking, intelligent, and had a good sense of humor. What did that imply about me? I had no answer for that either and wasn't about to bring it up to Meghan, so I put my arm around her waist as we walked.

After we got into the car, I called Raj to give him an update. "I'll get to Rover as soon as I can, but probably an hour at least. Don't leave before I get there."

15

Saturday Afternoon

It took nearly two hours before Meghan dropped me off at the Rover building. The only saving grace was the classic rock we listened to the whole ride back. Hours of singing classic rock songs had left us both in a good mood, even if a little hoarse. She went home to drop off her purchases. I'd pick her up later to go to Laney's house for trick-or-treating, and we'd get my costume on the way.

I walked through an empty hallway to my desk. The floor lights were off and the place was quiet. Raj had left a large suitcase sitting in the aisle between our cubicles. He was sitting at his desk illuminated by the light of his computer display.

Raj spoke as soon as he noticed me approaching. "I have to leave very soon."

"Oh, that's right. I forgot your flight home to India is tonight."

"Yes. I am very excited to visit my family. I beg pardon, how was Meghan?" Even under a time crunch, Raj was polite.

"Great. It was good to see her after she'd been gone all week. I wish she didn't have to travel so much for this new client of hers …" My voice trailed off. Meghan's last project hadn't ended smoothly, so she was happy to find another gig so quickly. She wasn't a fan of all the travel either. Business travel wasn't anyone's idea of fun.

"She has a lot of luggage," Raj said with a smirk.

"What? She only took one suitcase to New York," I said, confused by his comment.

"Oh, I mean she has a lot of baggage. That is the right saying, I think?" He seemed uncertain now.

"What do you mean? What's wrong with her? She seems normal to me." I'd enjoyed spending time with Meghan. Had Raj discovered something in her background that she hadn't shared with me?

Raj looked panicked at my reaction. "No, sorry. I meant only that she has a lot of experience in her job. Is that not what having a lot of baggage means?"

I laughed. Raj didn't often screw up his American idioms. "No, it doesn't mean that. But I'll let you look it up yourself." I sat down in Raj's guest chair. "Why don't you tell me what you've done so far?"

Raj spent the next few minutes updating me on his progress with the Santa Cruz County Sheriff's search warrant.

After he finished, I perched on the edge of his cube wall and summarized. "Okay, so Larry was a Rover customer." Good to know he supported my company. I resolved yet again to figure out how he had died and if someone had killed him. He'd have done the same for me.

Raj checked his watch and started fidgeting. Before he had to leave for the airport, I wrapped up. "But otherwise, he doesn't seem to have used Rover in the last few days before he died. He had no changes in his profile, no signs of stolen identity, etc."

"Precisely." Raj shut off his computer.

"Okay. You get to the airport. I've got it from here." I grew a little sad as I realized I'd miss Raj over the next few weeks. I liked him, enjoyed working near him, and looked forward to working together on our new project. I decided to tell him how I felt. "I'm glad it will finally be quiet around here while you're gone."

I continued teasing him as he packed up. "Hey, last chance for me to buy you a wedding present before you leave." This had been an ongoing topic of discussion for us over the last month. So many single Indian men working in Silicon Valley seemed to travel back home on an extended vacation and return married.

"Ha." Raj had told me he found this pattern funny as well. "Feel free to buy me a present, but no wedding for me." He picked up a little squishy ball bearing the logo of some long-forgotten software company and placed it on my desk. "Okay, now the ball is in your court." He grinned, pleased to sneak in one last idiom.

I nodded with appreciation. "That one cut the mustard. Now get out of here. I'll write the report for the police after I check out a few more things."

"Be careful," warned Raj. "Sometimes you do things that maybe you should not." On that cautionary note, he swung his backpack over his shoulder and pulled his suitcase along behind him down the empty corridor to the elevators.

No harm could come from double-checking a few comments I'd heard earlier this week. It wouldn't bring Larry back, but I would learn more about the people who would soon take over Rover. Besides, I was practically deputized as a law enforcement officer today, so it was the perfect opportunity for a little research.

I pulled up the Santa Clara County government website, then got frustrated upon learning that California privacy laws had eliminated online searching of governmental websites for most personal records, such as birth and death certificates, social security numbers, and marriage licenses. In general, I approved of stronger privacy laws, except when they hampered my own investigations.

Noticing a sentence on the bottom of the webpage that said summaries of civil court filings and results were still searchable online, I typed in a name and hit enter. The results didn't surprise me. To make sure the database was accurate, I tried my name. Again, no surprise. I tried the names of some of the folks I'd met recently, and, this time, one of the results did surprise me.

I leaned back in my chair, resting my lips against my steepled fingers. The pose was wasted, as no one was around to notice how much I resembled a detective engaged in deductive thinking. Despite my impressive appearance, I hadn't figured out anything except that people sometimes lied. *Big surprise there.*

In any case, posing like a detective didn't help me finish the report for the police. I began writing it but got confused trying to explain one of the details retained in our Rover customer ride database, so I logged in. Unlike the last time I used our database, I now had official permission. In fact, the search warrant practically meant I was legally obligated to access it. Almost giddy with power, I repeated one of the searches for Larry that Raj must have done, taking notes as I went. I pulled up Larry's address on our ride map. Our system zoomed in to his neighborhood and displayed the timestamp of the last ride from his house, which had taken place over two weeks ago. Raj had also confirmed that Larry had not used Rover anywhere else around the time of his death. I wrote a few more sentences in the report.

I stopped typing as a new idea struck me. To check it out, I extended the search of our ride map, snapping my fingers when something popped up on the screen that would help Larry's case. Mace would want to hear about this. And I would tell him ... right after I picked up something I needed from Larry's house. I smiled. It wasn't a pleasant smile, but again, no one was there to see me.

I wrapped up the report and sent it off before hurrying down the hallway. I was running late to pick up Meghan. We'd swing by Larry's house on our way to Laney's. If traffic wasn't too bad, we'd make it there well before the girls decided to leave for trick-

or-treating without me. In the elevator, I ordered a Rover car and texted Meghan that I was on my way.

As I waited outside the lobby door, my phone rang.

"Hey, Cuz. It's me. Sam."

As if anyone else called me that. "What's up? Are you at Laney's?" It was hard to hear anything other than the roar of street noise in the background. Convertibles had many appealing aspects, but a quiet ride wasn't one of them.

"Nah. I'm stuck in this godawful traffic. No one in this city can drive. It's like trying to park your car in Harvard Yard." Samantha enjoyed trying to develop her Boston accent. Whenever possible, she seemed to drop all her R's and lose other random consonants. All I heard was "pahk yuh cahr in hahvuhd yahd."

I yelled, "How late will you be?"

"Well, you don't have to holla. If I can make it through the next few blocks, hopefully we'll get moving and I'll get there soon. Tell Laney I'll be a little late."

I said okay and hung up. I didn't have the heart to tell her that the highway wouldn't get much faster until she'd cleared more of San Francisco, if she was lucky.

As I stepped into the Rover car, I was happy I didn't have to fight the San Francisco traffic every day. Living in the South Bay might not be as exciting, but I preferred the better weather, slightly better traffic, and …

I stopped trying to come up with more reasons why the South Bay was better than San Francisco and smiled as I remembered my own cleverness with the search warrant. Once he heard my report to the Santa Cruz deputies, Mace would be proud of me. Or at least he would be as soon as I grabbed what they needed from Larry's house.

*****

"Do you think I'm the reason they got together?" I blurted out as soon as Meghan joined me in the Rover car. I couldn't get the idea of Mace and Brody dating out of my head. They were so different.

She set down a plastic shopping bag, leaned over, and kissed me. "Hello and good to see you too." She laughed and then answered, "No, silly. Remember, Mace was already in that Starbucks store when we met him there that crazy night. He told us to come there, not the other way around."

I sat back in relief. She was right. They must have been a couple before I became a Starbucks regular. Otherwise, what would happen if both Brody and Mace wanted me to be their best man? That would be awkward. I didn't want to be part of either wedding party. Organizing bachelor parties would be too much work. Would they have separate bachelor parties? This was all too confusing for me. Of course, I would go to any potential wedding. Wedding cakes were extra good.

"Where are we going?" Meghan looked confused when the car didn't make the turn to Laney's house.

"I need to stop at Larry's house for a couple of minutes first to pick something up. It's not far out of the way."

"Your friend who died?"

"He was murdered. I'm helping the police figure out who did it."

"Marty ..." Meghan dragged out my name, her voice filled with a combination of doubt and disapproval.

"It's true. I was helping on the search warrant in the office when you dropped me off." I didn't explain that the search warrant was for Rover and not Larry's house. It was all part of the same investigation, wasn't it?

She either believed that I was part of the investigation ... or she accepted that this side trip meant only a short delay. Maybe she was getting used to me. I wasn't sure if that was a good thing.

When we pulled up to Larry's house, the Rover app told me the "Stay" feature was not available tonight. With the combination of Halloween parties and Saturday night, our cars were in high demand. Financially, that felt good, but it meant we would have to call for another Rover and Meghan couldn't leave her costume in the car.

The street was quiet, as if holding its breath before sunset and the official start of trick-or-treating. I breathed a sigh of relief that Gloria's car was missing from her driveway so she wouldn't catch me sneaking around the back. I stayed away from the front of Carmela's house to avoid her notice also. When I turned down the side path to Larry's backyard, Meghan stopped. "We're not going in the front?"

"Nope. You'll see." I snickered to myself.

When I grabbed the fake rock from the back porch and pulled out the key, Meghan stopped again and crossed her arms in concern. "Are you sure this is legal? You're sneaking in the back door with a key hidden inside a fake rock?"

"It's okay. Besides, I knew where his key was, didn't I?" *Thank you, Carmela.*

My knowledge and confidence must have convinced Meghan that I was legitimate. She uncrossed her arms and walked into the house while I held the door for her.

I smiled in anticipation of her reaction. Like the first time I went into Larry's house, she paused in the entrance as the impact hit her. "Oh, that poor man." Meghan grabbed my forearm. "Was he getting help?"

"Uh ... I don't know. I don't think so." I had focused on how Meghan would react to the surprise rather than consider how my friend had hidden a big issue from his friends. That wasn't cool.

There had to be a support group for this sort of thing. I committed to making a donation to them in Larry's honor.

I took Meghan's hand and walked her through the maze until we reached the stacks of Sirius Innovation materials. Unlike me during my first visit, Meghan wasn't motivated to pick up old articles along the way and start reading.

I found the most recent folder lying on top of the second stack. Picking it up, I started flipping through it, searching for the item that had tickled my memory.

The front door rattled, startling a gasp out of Meghan and causing me to drop the folder.

Meghan started toward the door and yelled, "Coming," before noticing the piles blockading access to it.

I quickly shushed her with a hiss.

Her eyebrows knitted together as she took a step back toward me. In a whisper, she asked, "So the truth is, you're not supposed to be in here?"

"Not exactly," I admitted, starting to sweat.

She frowned at my admission before we heard more noises from the porch. I heard keys rattling outside as something pushed against the old door. But Larry was dead. Had his ghost returned to haunt his old house on Halloween? Why would a ghost need keys?

I shook my head and hurriedly bent over to gather the papers back into the folder. A few pieces had fallen in the aisle on the other side. Getting to them took us around two more bends in the maze.

Crouching on the ground, Meghan grabbed one of the papers while I picked up the other and stuffed them both back into the manila folder.

The ghost turned the key to unbolt the front door.

Somehow neither Meghan nor I screamed. I might have gasped aloud, though, so I didn't hear if Meghan did the same.

"We gotta get out of here," I said. I wasn't interested in meeting whatever was at the front door. I'd call the police when we got away.

Still in a crouch, Meghan scrambled away in the wrong direction. I whispered her name, but she didn't hear me.

Remaining hunched over, I hurried to follow her.

The maze led us away from both the front and kitchen doors. Meghan tripped as she ran into the stairs but broke her fall with her hands.

We could hear the creak of the front door as it opened for the first time in a while. It opened only a few inches before running into the piles of junk.

On hands and knees, we scrambled up the stairs.

No rational thoughts went through my mind. I only knew I wanted to be away from here, from the ghost. What kind of idiots went into the dark, overstuffed house of a dead man? On Halloween. This was how horror movies started. Before people started dying.

Meghan reached the top of the stairs and turned down the hall.

The front door flew open as the ghost's mighty shove pushed over stacks of junk.

My back couldn't take all this hunching over and scrambling, so I straightened up as I followed Meghan. I looked over my shoulder right before turning the corner.

I caught a glimpse of something, or someone, dressed all in black with a black mask covering their face and head. I sucked in my breath and, in my surprise, almost ran into the wall. My brief glimpse of the intruder had revealed what looked like a ninja climbing over the piles by the front door.

My panic grew.

Ninjas were chasing us. Those were worse than ghosts. We might only have minutes left to live. Ninjas had throwing stars and were crazy fast. In feudal Japan, ninjas had been the world's best assassins and spies.

Now one was after us. Didn't they travel in packs?

Meghan located a bedroom and jumped inside.

I followed and locked the door behind me. How long would a simple lock hold off ninjas who were after us? "Ninjas!" I said to Meghan, trying to catch my breath.

"What?" Looking up from her exploration of the window seat, she shook her head, confused.

"We have to get out of here."

"Ya think?" Meghan's sarcastic tone was new. It was her only outward sign of nervousness as she glanced around the room, undoubtedly searching for a ninjatō, a ninja sword.

I opened the closet, looking for any suitable weapons.

"Marty, stop fooling around and come help." Meghan leaned against the wall, trying to jimmy open the stuck window.

More piles of junk crashed downstairs. I double-checked that the door was locked on my way over to Meghan.

When I turned around, Meghan was standing outside the window on the slanted roof. She waved urgently for me to follow her.

Despite the last few chaotic minutes, Meghan had managed to hold onto her plastic costume bag. She was good in a crisis. Handing her the folder, which she put into the bag, I clambered out onto the roof. Heights were not my thing. Plus, there were slippery leaves that could lead to my death or dismemberment. I took a deep breath to steady myself and get my bearings. A few feet away from the house and right below us, Larry's pool glimmered in the darkening sky.

"Marty, go, go, go," Meghan implored me urgently.

I did what I was told.

I jumped off the roof into the pool.

When I surfaced, I spit out the stale, disgusting water that I'd swallowed and swept aside the wet leaves in front of my face. At least the deep end of the pool had been closest to that bedroom.

Looking up, I saw Meghan still standing on the roof with her hands held up and out to her sides. Her face reflected a mixture of dismay and respect for my death-defying act, although her expression could have simply been utter amazement.

Then she carefully climbed down the fire escape rope ladder that she had unfurled against the house.

As I climbed out of the cold pool, she gave a hard flip of her wrists and the rope ladder detached from the window and fell to the ground.

Together, we hurried to the back of the yard, using an old tree stump to climb over the fence. The last thing we wanted to do was try to get back around the side of the house before the ninja could beat us to the front door.

Water streamed off me as I straddled the fence, my teeth chattering and my getaway far less graceful than Meghan's. As I scrambled over the fence, I looked back at Larry's house.

Standing in the open window with hands on hips, the ninja stared at me.

Worried about ninja poison darts or throwing stars, I didn't bother climbing down as I dropped to the safety of the backyard neighbor's house. Although I fell to my hands and knees, we'd escaped death.

This time.

But that all-black apparition did not look happy.

16

Saturday Evening

"Marty, hurry," said Meghan from halfway across the yard as she ran toward the street.

And I ran.

I ran so far away.

I just ran ... because baby, we were born to run.

We stopped running three blocks away. Although Meghan didn't seem affected by our near-marathon, I had no endurance.

As I stood puffing, with my hands on my knees, Meghan asked, "So, now will you go to the gym with me?"

Resistance was futile. I'd always wanted to work a famous *Star Trek* line into normal conversation, but this didn't seem like the right moment, so I nodded instead, still too winded to speak anyway. I pulled out my phone and requested a Rover, then handed the phone to Meghan to put in her bag. Leaving it sitting in my soaking wet jeans would only tempt fate. My phone was supposed to be waterproof, but not all engineers were as good as me.

"You jumped off the roof so we'd get down faster? That was pretty brave. Really stupid and dangerous, but brave." Meghan kissed my cheek, bending at the waist to avoid getting wet.

I decided not to tell her that I hadn't noticed the escape ladder until after I had jumped. While I had been panicking in the bedroom looking for a ninjatō sword to fight off the ninja, she had located a fire escape ladder, opened the stuck window, attached the ladder to the window frame, and climbed out onto the ledge. Ninjas had a way of nullifying my powers of observation.

"I never knew you could detach escape ladders from below. How'd you know so much about them?" I asked her as we waited in the shadows near a darkened house. No sense making us easy for a ninja to spot.

Meghan snorted. "I don't think you're supposed to be able to do that, but you've heard some of the stories about my brothers. Growing up, I learned a whole range of useful, and perhaps not mainstream, skills." Her eyes glinted in the dark.

I resolved to avoid meeting her brothers for as long as possible. I tried calling Mace from the Rover car, but he didn't answer. Hopefully he was merely busy and not blocking my calls. To stay on the safe side, I left him a two-word voicemail: "Call me." Even I couldn't screw up that message.

When we knocked on Laney's door, Megan, my niece, opened it holding an empty candy wrapper. Before she could speak, we slid inside, then I turned around and bolted the door. No ninjas were going to waltz in Laney's front door without an effort.

Megan finished chewing and said, "Hi, Uncle Marty. Meghan. Betcha can't guess what I am?"

Her habit of betting on everything was getting expensive for me. If I lost a bet, I had to pay her a dollar. Even if I won, I didn't seem to come out ahead. Similar to Las Vegas odds. I took a closer look at her. This was an easy bet, so I took the gamble. "You're a shark. Gray felt costume with a pointy head and tail. Wait, I'll bet you're the San Jose Sharks mascot. What's his name? Oh yeah, Sharkie." I started to put out my hand for a high five.

"Uncle Marty." Megan's face dropped as she fought back tears.

Then I noticed the white horn coming out of her hood and made a rapid adjustment. "Oh, sorry. I didn't see the horn. Of course, you're a unicorn." I extended my hand all the way. I'd crushed this bet.

"I'm a narwhal." She stomped her foot before rushing off down the hallway, trying not to cry in front of us.

"Well done, Uncle Marty," commented Meghan with a half-smile and a single raised eyebrow.

The ninja episode must have rattled me more than I thought. It was unlike me to miss a detail, especially something like a horn.

"She's a tough one," Meghan added in a soft voice. "Let me go put on my costume in the bathroom while you take your foot out of the narwhal's mouth."

Perhaps I should explain to my niece that the unicorn guess wasn't so far off the mark since narwhals were sometimes called "the unicorn of the sea." Was this the right moment for an Uncle Marty lecture? I considered my options as I walked to her room.

Before I reached it, Laney hobbled out of Skye's bedroom, her foot still in the soft cast. "You're late. And Sam's late. Is it too much to ask that you be on time for Halloween? It's one night a year." She took stock of my appearance. "And why are you dripping all over my floor? Why would you go swimming now? And no costume? Here." She handed me a towel from the nearby dryer. "You can go trick-or-treating as a wet blanket."

This wasn't my first time being around a stressed-out Laney, so I knew enough not to react. "I'll take a quick shower and then Meghan and I can take the girls out."

"Fine. I'm taking them down the block first." She pointed an emphatic finger at me. "I've always taken them trick-or-treating, and this … this isn't going to stop me tonight." She hobbled to her bedroom to get me some of her late husband's old sweats. She must have kept some of his stuff around as a reminder. Plus, you never knew when old sweats would come in handy.

Skye stepped into the hallway from her room and gave me a small wave.

I smiled when I saw her costume—a Hawaiian shirt and shorts with a small purse at her waist. "Hi, Skye. I like your engineer's costume. Was that inspired by me?" I felt proud that in only a few months, I'd had such a big impact on her life.

She rolled her eyes and sighed. "I'm a tourist. This is a fanny pack." She flipped her hair in disgust and turned her back on me. Then, closing her bedroom door with a backward fling of her hand, she left me standing alone in the hall. Rather than trying again with Megan and extending my losing streak, I walked back to the living room and sat down.

A few minutes later, Megan wandered back into the kitchen without speaking to me. She slid over to the candy bowl, grabbed a few pieces, and stuffed them into her mouth. Megan was a practical girl. She saw no sense in waiting to walk around the block when candy was sitting out in her own kitchen. Megan lay down on the couch across from me and continued to ignore me while she chewed. I stepped into the kitchen and grabbed a few pieces of candy for myself.

After only a few minutes of us chewing candy and me dripping pool water on the floor, Meghan announced her return by placing the folder I took from Larry's house on the kitchen table and the bag with her regular clothes on the floor, then paraded into the living room, twirling to show off her costume. She had my full attention. She wore a pirate outfit—a sexy, low-cut pirate dress with a long slit up the side and long black boots that I'd never seen before. To complete the look, she had a fake parrot sewn onto the shoulder of her dress.

With a broad smile, I looked her in the eyes and winked. "I like your toucan."

"That's a parrot, Uncle Marty," said Megan with a disgusted

scoff. "Don't you know anything about animals? Toucans are much bigger than parrots."

"And not as good-looking," I added.

Meghan smiled back at me and then left to help Laney and Skye.

Before taking a fast shower, I tried Mace again. I needed to talk to him about Larry and the ninja and what I'd found in the folder and my online search. No answer, and this time I didn't leave a message. I couldn't afford to frustrate him now. I needed his help, so I gave up and headed for the shower.

In Megan's bedroom, I got dressed in the old sweatpants and T-shirt from Laney while pondering my last-minute costume options. The art supplies and other items scattered around the room gave me an idea.

When I came out of the bedroom, everyone was waiting for me in the living room.

After taking one look at me, Laney asked, "What on earth are you supposed to be?"

I looked down proudly at the cardboard sign hanging around my neck with "I love ceilings" written in a careful hand. I held one of Megan's pom-poms up like a cheerleader and said, "I'm a ceiling fan." When no one responded, I asked, "Get it? Go ceilings go! Ceiling fan ..." My voice trailed off as I noticed their faces.

Laney got to her feet. "We better get out of here, girls, before his attempts at humor make us sick." While the girls rushed to grab their pumpkins, Laney added, "Samantha texted that she'll be here soon. I can only make it around the block and then she'll keep me company while you two take the girls out for a longer round."

Before she shut the door behind her, Laney paused, her hand on the doorknob, and glared at the dog. "Make sure Buddy doesn't get out of the house. And watch him so he doesn't turn on the gas on the stove. Again." With a final frown, she headed out into the night with the girls.

A moment later the doorbell rang. "Now what?" I asked, in perhaps not the nicest tone, as I flung open the door.

A large crowd of young trick-or-treaters quieted by my shout stood staring at me. Understandable, as the kids were supposed to speak first, not have the adult yell at them as he opened the door.

Meghan stepped into the breach. "Happy Halloween!"

That soothed the crowd of youngsters, and everyone chimed, "Trick or treat."

We had done it in reverse order, but it sufficed. There must have been twenty kids in that first group. Meghan got busy greeting a continuing influx of costumed little ones as even more kids approached on the sidewalk.

"Marty, we're almost out of this batch of candy. Go get the other bag. Laney said it was in the garage." Meghan stepped out onto the porch and pulled the door shut behind her to prevent the curious Buddy from escaping.

I almost reminded her that she needed to wait for the kids to ring the doorbell, but after my earlier performance, I wasn't about to instruct her on how to do Halloween right. Wondering how much candy my niece Megan had snagged already tonight, I walked through the kitchen and out into the garage to search for the next bag of candy.

It took me a while to locate it. The warm weather must have led Laney to store the bags of candy in her garage refrigerator to keep them from melting. I ripped open a bag and did a taste test. Quality control. Then, I flipped off the garage light and stepped back into the kitchen.

The ninja was standing at the other side of Laney's kitchen table.

I froze. A bag of candy wouldn't ward off a ninja for long.

Locked in place, I watched as the ninja used a gloved hand to withdraw a small spray can from the pocket of their black sweatshirt.

The ninja pointed the can at me with one hand while using the other to gesture for me to hand over the folder from Larry's house that lay on the table in front of me.

I wasn't surprised at the lack of speech. After all, ninjas didn't talk. They were silent assassins. My eyes focused on the menace. Not a shooting star, poison dart, or sword—instead, the ninja was threatening me with a can of pepper spray. And not any old can, but the most famous brand ever—Mace.

Of course.

I had no choice. Pepper spray was supposed to be wickedly painful. And who knew what other dangerous weapons the ninja held in reserve if I survived a spraying?

Wishing I'd taken a photo of the contents earlier, I picked up the folder, then took a tentative step closer and held out my arm to the ninja.

A tan blur whizzed past me and launched into the air.

Sixty pounds of speeding Buddy hit the unsuspecting ninja square in the chest.

The ninja dropped to the ground, flattened by Buddy better than any of the 49ers' safeties tackled their opponents.

Finding my voice, I yelled and leapt forward. Gang-tackling ninjas did not violate any rules. The ninja was strong, but Buddy had dealt a stunning blow, and I was bigger. After a brief scramble, I knocked away the pepper spray.

Hearing my shout through the open windows, Meghan rushed back inside the house. "Marty!" she yelled before joining the melee.

During the struggle, the ninja ended up facedown before going limp.

We'd disarmed a ninja!

Keeping a wary eye out for any sudden moves, I leaned forward. With all the skills I'd picked up from years of watching cop shows and superhero movies, I kept my weight on the ninja's back while I reached over and yanked off the mask.

The mask came off, revealing Peri Syte, the fawning HR woman from Sirius. I shouldn't have been so surprised.

"Get off me already, I can't breathe," Peri huffed.

Buddy returned and licked her face. He wanted to play again.

"Gross. Let me up," Peri demanded.

I stayed where I was, my knees on her back. I never liked her anyway.

While Meghan was searching the garage for something to tie up Peri, I called Mace. He answered this time. He had that superhero timing to sense when he was most needed, and victory was at hand. I told him to get over to Laney's right away because we'd caught a ninja in her house. Then I hung up to focus on keeping pressure on a squirming Peri.

With some nylon rope she found in the garage, Meghan tied Peri's arms behind her back. Meghan gave the rope some extra twists to make sure our makeshift handcuffs stayed in place.

The police must have been in the neighborhood, because they arrived with startling speed. Meghan managed to let them in the unlocked front door before they smashed it open.

The police cars' flashing lights flickered across the inside of the house as four officers flooded into the kitchen and took over for me.

Before we could even start to explain what happened, two more police cars squealed to a stop outside our house, and a fire truck's distinctive siren sounded in the distance.

Sergeant Jackson burst into the room, moving faster than I'd ever seen him move before. "What happened? Where's Marty? What did he do?"

17

Later Saturday Evening

"Everything is okay now that you're here," said Meghan. "Thanks for coming so fast." She directed her words to the veritable army of police officers in the house.

"Good. Why don't you sit down over here and tell me what happened?" Mace pulled two kitchen chairs to the side and gestured for Meghan to sit next to him as he took out his pen and notebook.

I'm fine too, thank you, Sergeant. I started speaking before Meghan could answer. "She"—I pointed to Peri—"killed Larry. And tried to kill us too."

"I did not. You broke into Larry's house." Peri lifted her head. She wasn't going down without dragging me into the mud, too. She strained against the cuffs, rubbing her arms together as she tried to free herself.

Mace stopped the bickering with a look and commanded, "Quiet." Even his fellow police officers halted what they were doing. The sergeant looked skeptical as he pointed at me. "Explain."

I didn't hesitate. "After we got the search warrant, Raj and I checked Rover's records. Larry didn't take a Rover last Friday or

Saturday, or any time in the last week. After Raj left for the airport, I expanded the search."

"You violated the terms of the search warrant?" Mace's rumble turned threatening.

I swallowed hard but stood my ground and justified my actions. At least, I hoped I did. "Well, I'd call it more of a difference in interpretation of the terms. The warrant did authorize searches for use of Rover at or near Larry Cohen's residence."

Mace's eyebrows knit together in a dangerous manner. I finished, "And I found something." I looked around the room to check if the other officers were watching.

Unappreciative of my dramatic pause, Mace said, "Out with it already."

"Last Saturday morning, a Rover car picked up someone around the corner from Larry's house." My search had yielded this unexpected result. Cautious of Mace's reaction, I cut short my next dramatic pause. Those worked on all the TV cop shows, but Mace didn't work from the standard script. He was a different kind of action hero, one beyond the Hollywood norms.

I got back to my point before he stuck something pointy in me. "The client that Rover picked up was Peri Syte, head of HR for Sirius Innovation." Pointing an accusatory finger toward her in triumph, I added, "She's the ninja right there in handcuffs, and she also—"

The front door slammed open. "That's it! That dog is out of here," Laney panted from the doorway, leaning on her good leg with Skye and Megan standing behind her.

The nearest cops had started to draw their weapons and move toward her when Mace waved them off. "Ms. Tran, everything's fine now."

She almost growled in response. "Now? What did he do this time?"

"Marty? Oh, you mean your dog. He didn't do anything—"

I interrupted, "No, he did. Buddy totally saved the day. He tackled the ninja. She got in the house and threatened me with Mace."

Laney threw up both hands in confusion, nearly smacking Skye in the face. "What ninja? Why did Sergeant Jackson threaten you?"

"Not that Mace—"

"Stop!" Sergeant Jackson used his command voice again.

Meghan, always clear-headed, came to the rescue. "The woman in the black clothes broke into the house. She threatened Marty with a can of pepper spray. Buddy tackled her. Then Marty and I captured her and tied her up. I called 9-1-1 and Marty must have called Sergeant Jackson, then everyone showed up." She stood, brought her chair over so Laney could sit, and took a deep breath. "There, now we're all caught up."

She walked over to me and took my hand. No one else could tell the experience had shaken her too, but I could feel her trembling, so I wrapped my arm around her and tried to calm us both down.

Mace returned to his interrogation. "Taking a Rover might be crazy, but it isn't illegal," he said to me. "What does it matter if she was picked up near his house? He wasn't home. This sounds like another of your crazy ideas."

I resented that comment. Only some of my ideas were crazy. "She lied to me." At Mace's look of disbelief, I quickly added, "And Raj. He was there, too. We were in Portland at the Sirius office when we met her on Monday morning. Peri told us she had been in San Francisco all day on Saturday with her husband. But she wasn't." Administering the final coup de grâce, I added, "And she was divorced two years ago. I found her divorce decree online. She was here in San Jose in the late morning, not in San Francisco. That's plenty of time to make it to the mountains, kill Larry, and come back."

All eyes turned to Peri. Her face tightened and her eyes shifted as she searched for an excuse but found nothing.

On a roll, I continued, "You'll want to see this, too." I picked up the folder from the kitchen table and handed it to Mace.

"What's this?" he rumbled as he opened it and began thumbing through the contents.

I stood up a little straighter. "Underneath the printout of Peri's weekly calendar is a signature form opening up an offshore brokerage account. It authorizes stock option trading, starting with a large order of put options for Sirius Innovation."

Sergeant Jackson gave me a puzzled look. "It's signed 'Patti Smith.' What does that have to do with anything?"

"That's Peri's signature. She signed us in at Sirius on Monday. The signature has large loopy letters and the I's have hearts in place of the dots. Looks like a little girl's signature, right?"

"It is not!" Peri's eyes darted bolts at me, and she jerked her shoulder forward as she squirmed again. "People have made fun of my signature for my whole life. It's not a little girl's signature, it's just feminine."

Sergeant Jackson ignored her for the moment. "What's a put option?" he asked me.

"It gives you the right to sell a stock at a given price." The blank looks in the room led me to explain further, "Basically, it's a bet that the stock price will drop. If you own a put option, you make a lot of money fast if the stock drops. She bought a lot of put options on Sirius and would make a mint if their stock plummeted. She's an exec there. That's illegal."

Sergeant Jackson craned his neck to the side and rubbed the top of his crew cut. "Okay …"

I could tell he wasn't sure what to do next. That's what partners were for.

"Arrest Peri Syte for killing Larry." If I ever spoke in a courtroom, that would have to become my courtroom voice. I continued, "Larry had this signed form in his house. It's proof she was breaking the law. She killed him and then tried to steal it back to cover her tracks."

Mace moved his hand to his chin. "Well, we can bring her in for breaking and entering. Our financial crimes unit will need to talk to her, but there's no proof of murder in what you've said."

Peri squirmed again, rubbing her arms against her side, and this time a cop grabbed her wrists to still her. "Let me scratch myself, you doofus." She almost spat on him in her annoyance. "I'm not trying to escape. Only a moron would do that in a room full of cops."

Her repeated movements prickled my memory. "Hey, pull up the arm of her sweatshirt," I told the cop.

The cop looked at Mace, who nodded. He'd noticed Peri's odd movements as well.

The officer pulled up the sleeve of her black sweatshirt, revealing an arm that was bright red and blotchy from repeated scratching.

I stepped closer for a better look. "Hey! You've got that same burn with little dots on your arm as Larry did." I breathed in sharply. "You were there. You did kill him." It hadn't seemed real until now.

Mace leaned in for a better look. "That does look awfully similar," he said tentatively. A sunburn wasn't enough to convince him.

"She had Larry's keys," Meghan said softly.

Mace glanced at Meghan.

I jumped on that. "Yeah. Meghan's right. How could she have them unless she drove his car back from the mountains—after leaving him dead in the forest."

Mace nodded. He shifted gears, and his officer's voice returned as he looked at Peri. "Ma'am, you're under arrest—"

Peri interrupted him with a half-sob, half-laugh. "I didn't kill him. That idiot … He grabbed a Giant Hogweed plant with his bare hands and thrust it into my hands when I wasn't looking. That fool told me, 'It's the world's biggest flower for you.'" She sniffed and her eyes teared up. "What a romantic fool." She shook her head. "I didn't kill him, but I was there."

Everyone froze, not daring to interrupt.

She continued, her voice pleading. "I told him to drop it. I mean, what idiot doesn't know those plants are toxic. They can burn you. Thirty minutes later, I started feeling itchy. Larry did too, but more. His rash came on so fast." She shook a little. "His hands, arms, and face got all red and then he fell down, complaining he couldn't breathe. He got frantic. He kept looking around for his EpiPen." Her voice cracked. "He didn't have it with him. He gave me his keys, and I ran back to his car. His EpiPen bag was on the floor." She shook her head sadly. "When I got back to him with the bag, he was dead." She shuddered, and a tear dripped down her cheek. "That's all. It was so sad."

"So sad," I repeated in a soft voice, almost to myself.

Meghan leaned in and wrapped both arms around me, pulling me in closer and squeezing my waist in sympathy.

At first, I felt sorry for Peri too. Then I got mad. "No!" I said emphatically, startling the room. I pulled loose from Meghan. "That's not all." I shook my finger at Peri as I made a litany of accusations. "You didn't call 9-1-1 to try to save Larry. You drove his car back to his house without telling anyone. You snuck around the corner to take a Rover home so no one would know you were there. You used scary ninja skills to follow us here and snuck into this house to get that document back." I punctuated each comment with a stab of my finger at her.

The tears in her eyes dried up, replaced by angry bolts of lightning aimed straight at me.

Ninja death rays! I overcame my momentary terror to finish my accusations. "You even had an affair with Doug Samerson and went with him to the Cayman Islands to open illegal accounts together."

Peri recoiled, her nose wrinkling. "Nasty." She tried to spit the bad taste out of her mouth. Her reaction had been spontaneous. No one was that good an actor.

Perhaps I had misread that situation. I tried to recover my previous momentum. "Well, you're no innocent bystander anyway. Larry died because of you and then you covered it up so you wouldn't get caught. All for money." I continued pointing at her as the room absorbed the full impact of the story. Suddenly I wondered if Larry had known about the stock options. Had he figured out who had signed the form? Was he in on it with Peri?

I felt deflated. The moment of appreciative silence in the room was all too brief before a familiar voice spoke.

"Wow, Cuz." Samantha stood behind Laney with her hands on both girls' shoulders. She must have arrived unnoticed.

Her approval felt good. I couldn't often impress my cousin, especially in person. I nodded, feeling better. "Pretty impressive detecting, huh?"

"No, I mean that's the weakest excuse for a Halloween costume I've ever seen."

Skye and Megan snorted. With muffled chuckles, the officers snapped out of their daze as well.

"Hang on," Laney said to Peri with a frown. "I don't have the same last name as Marty. How'd you find my house?"

The room quieted as everyone's eyes shifted back to Peri, who sneered at Laney. "I'm in HR. We know things."

Laney's glare intensified, and she opened her mouth as if to set the record straight that she too was part of that secret society.

Peri didn't let her interrupt, adding, "Marty put you down as his emergency contact when he registered at Sirius. His apartment was dark so I guessed he might have gone here. He sure wasn't heading straight to a party after jumping into the pool."

My mouth fell open. She'd been to my apartment?

Mace had heard enough. He started reading Peri her rights.

"That's my pom-pom," Megan announced to the room of officers, pointing out my possession of her property, looking for someone to rectify the situation or possibly even arrest me.

A few officers merely chuckled at her indignant hands-on-hips pose. They recognized a borrowed pom-pom when they saw one.

Samantha's purse dinged, and she pulled out a phone before noticing it was Izzy's. Her face dropped.

I stepped over to console her. Although I felt more settled now that Larry's death was solved, Izzy's death was still fresh to Samantha.

The phone buzzed again as an image flashed on the screen.

Samantha recoiled in disgust as she scrambled to throw it back in her purse.

"Wait. Let me see that again," I said.

"Eww." Using only two fingers to avoid touching the screen, Samantha handed it to me.

I looked at the photo of a man's hand holding his pants open to reveal more than I cared to see.

Then it clicked for me.

"Mace … I mean Sergeant Jackson," I corrected as he bristled in front of the other officers gathered around Peri. "Look at this." I showed him the unlocked phone.

"What is this?" Although Mace wasn't pleased with my interruption, I'd earned a little consideration.

"This guy's been sending sexts, you know, explicit photos, to Isabella Hernandez. That's the woman from Sirius who was killed at the parachuting competition in Hollister." His eyes tightened in impatience, so I finished quickly, "I know who's doing it."

His jaw clenched, any traces of tolerance for my dramatic pauses gone.

I got on with it already. "It's Alan. An IT guy from Sirius."

Samantha got upset. "Wait! A guy from Izzy's job sent her those gross texts for months? What a creep! How do you know?"

"What did you say?" Peri grew agitated as she leaned toward me. "Do you mean Alan Johnson?" Reacting to my confusion, she added, "Our tech security guy, Alan. You met him in Portland outside Vince's office."

I nodded. I hadn't known his last name yet recognized his distinctive bright orange watch band. You didn't see many of those around.

Peri exploded. "That son of a—"

Laney interrupted, "Hey! My kids are here."

Peri swallowed her curse. "For months?" She stopped and then took a deep breath. "All this time when we were together?" Jerking out of the cop's grasp, she lunged toward me.

Two officers caught up to her, but she'd already stopped in front of me. That was a good thing, as I hadn't budged. I was still rooted to the spot, staring at Peri. Engineers were hired for their brains, not their reflexes.

With her hands still cuffed behind her back, she leaned over to look at the sext. When she saw his wrist band clearly visible in the corner, she moaned, "We were in love." Her voice cracked. "At least he told me he was in love with me. We were going to get married as soon as …"

Peri shook herself as another wave of anger swept across her face. "That … that—"

"Children!" Laney interrupted again.

Laney's parenting approach confused me. She was fine with her girls standing in the same room with a killer but not with them hearing a curse word.

Peri looked up at Mace, her eyes dark and burning. "It was all Alan's idea." She looked like she wanted to spit when she used his name. "Alan stole Samerson's email password and read his emails. When he found out our new drug trial was failing, he wanted us to buy puts against Sirius with fake accounts, move to Vanuatu, and live by the beach."

"Va-new-a-who?" asked Mace.

"It's an island in the South Pacific." Peri sighed. "It sounded so romantic." Then, her eyes widened as she drew in a sudden breath. "He was flirting with Izzy, wasn't he? I thought he hung around Samerson and Peters to steal company secrets." She gritted her teeth. "But he was there to flirt with her ... that floozy. That—"

"Kids!" came Laney's sharp voice.

"Hey!" complained Samantha about the depiction of her friend.

Peri darted an annoyed glance at Laney but complied. Taking a deep breath to control her emotions, she returned to her story. "Alan said Larry called Izzy late on Friday when he was fiddling with something in Samerson's office. He couldn't hear much except it was about the drug trial. He wanted me to ask Larry out, you know, on a pretend date, to find out what he'd told Izzy."

Then her eyes narrowed as her suspicions crystallized. "Wait a minute. Yeah." She looked directly at Mace. "I think he did it. I think Alan killed Izzy. That ..." Glancing at Laney, she stopped herself this time. "I forgot Alan told me he'd follow up with Izzy. It's been so busy with my arm and getting ready to leave the country next week. I thought he meant he'd ask her what she'd heard. He's sick. Sending sexts to a woman he killed."

She turned back to Mace. "You should check Alan's computer and look for any videos of him in Hollister. He was watching all these videos about parachutes. I'll bet he found something and messed with her parachute. Now he's trying to cover his tracks by sending those gross pictures, that—"

This time Mace stopped her and asked Laney for some paper. He kicked everyone out of the kitchen except the police and Peri. From the living room, I watched as he took off Peri's cuffs and handed her a pen. He asked her to write down her story in detail right away. While she wrote, he placed an officer on guard, then stepped into the garage to make a phone call.

I sat on the couch, catching my breath while the cops stood

around. Meghan, Samantha, Laney, and the girls went out to the porch to hand out candy. Buddy padded up in front of me and placed his head underneath my hand. "Just covering your bases in case Laney decides to kick you out after all, huh?" I whispered to him as I stroked his head.

No one noticed me petting tonight's hero.

Mace came out of the garage after a few minutes. "Our APB caught Mr. Johnson at the airport. He had checked in for an international flight. TSA is holding him."

"Alan was leaving today? Without me?" Peri gasped and made small stuttering sounds. "I'll testify against him. I'll totally testify. He did it. I'm sure he killed her. How could I be so stupid?" She put her head down on her arms and cried.

After a few minutes, she stopped crying, picked up her pen, and, with a vengeance, finished writing.

Buddy had enough of hanging out with me. He wandered away in search of new trouble, or food.

Peri threw her pen down on the table. "There." She looked up at the nearest officer and, with a cold edge to her voice, asked, "Can they torture him before his execution?"

Before the officers escorted Peri out of the house, one more silly question bugged me. "Why all the way to Vanuatu? Wouldn't it be easier to go somewhere like the Cayman Islands?" As she started gagging again, I added, "Not with Samerson, but isn't it closer?"

Peri gave a disgusted snort. "There's no extradition to the US from Vanuatu like there is from the Caymans. Besides, where'd you think Alan got the idea for the options trading? He's good on the technical crap, but he's not that smart. Well, at least he knew he didn't need to fly to the Caymans, or Vanuatu, to open a secret account for illegal stock trading. Samerson is so stupid. You just need bitcoin, a fake email account, and a burner phone, and you're all set. Samerson used his company email to set up the appointments and then thought deleting the emails would erase them." She shook her head in disbelief. "Honestly, Samerson is such an idiot."

At that, Mace left her with the other officers and stepped out to make another phone call. When he returned, he gave me a nod of grudging respect.

I'd take it. We were as good as partners again!

A few minutes later, I traded places with Laney and the girls as they went inside for a family meeting. I stood on the porch with Meghan and Samantha, watching Peri scowl at me from the back seat of the police car as it pulled away from the curb. She wasn't so scary now that her ninja powers had fizzled out. The fire truck had long gone, and the other officers had turned off their cars' flashers as they finished their paperwork.

It was a good thing I didn't have to figure out how to write up all of tonight's adventures. I'd leave it to the news reports to inform the Rover execs that the Sirius acquisition had gone down in flames. Best not to have the Rover leadership associate my name with this fiasco. I resolved to get into work on Monday extra early. The discussions about what happened to Sirius should prove most interesting.

Sirius' execs wanted too much, too fast. Silicon Valley was like that sometimes. Samerson was soon going to have a whole new group of people to listen to his stories. He, Peri, and Alan could experience how well that "Winning Together" value would be received in prison. Although not an exec, Alan had wanted to make a killing too. He just did it the wrong way.

After my up-close look at Sirius management, the Rover leadership no longer seemed so terrible. Not that I'd tell them that, of course. After all, engineers had to keep their distance. Management was an entirely different species.

I was still excited that the Rover leadership had approved my proposal for a new service offering. Now, it looked like I'd get a chance to implement it right away without having to get the Sirius leadership team to approve it too. Although the Rover execs didn't give me a bonus or raise, they promised me a big stock option grant if things went well. And they would.

The impact of my successful presentation hadn't sunk in yet. So much had happened in the last thirty-six hours that I couldn't believe my presentation had taken place only yesterday morning. We'd start our testing on Monday. Our latest engineering hire, Fernando, would join me for the beta project, and Raj would complete our little team when he got back from India. I'd get to work with an old friend and a new friend—one who made great barbeque. *One was silver and the other gold.* That was the only part of the lyrics I remembered from my brief Girl Scouting adventure. That and the definition of B.I.F.F.Y. I shuddered.

Everything was returning to normal. Even better than normal.

I smiled and took Meghan's hand while Samantha tossed out handfuls of candy to the few trick-or-treaters left. Even Mace seemed more relaxed, almost content, as he greeted the kids who paraded past. At least his voice didn't seem to frighten them. He stood next to Samantha, not speaking to us, but not angry either.

The front door opened and Laney, Megan, and Skye filed back outside onto the crowded porch with the rest of us. The other cops stood chatting near their cars.

"We decided," announced Megan, putting both hands on her hips.

"… on the design for Sunshine 2," added Skye, providing much-needed context.

"Thank God." I couldn't believe they'd taken this long to finalize the color of Laney's new car. "I'm so done hearing all your arguments about it. What is it?"

Taking advantage of the pause during their indecision over who should tell us, Megan grabbed a piece of candy from the basket and stuffed it in her mouth before Laney could stop her. My niece had an impressive ability to inhale candy and remove the wrappers at the same time.

Before anyone could speak, a sports car roared up the block, going far too fast and disturbing the now peaceful neighborhood nearing the end of Halloween night. As the car approached us, the driver noticed all the police cars outside our house and jammed on the brakes.

As the car slid past the house, I gasped and paled. The driver was the same delivery guy from earlier in the week, and there were two more gang members in the car. They stared out at us from their open windows, frowning and clearly dissatisfied as they took in the spectacle of cops, police cars, and the crowd on the porch.

The driver must have regained his senses, because the car accelerated away with a loud roar that rattled the house. Two of the quicker cops had jumped into the street to catch the license plate, but the back bumper was empty.

Why had they come? Why were there no plates? Were they going to kill me? Kidnap me? I stood there, not breathing. Five weeks had gone by without any sign of the South American gang. I figured I'd escaped with only a scare. If only I hadn't ordered that takeout dinner on Tuesday!

Mace, recognizing the signs of a gang car, swiveled his head from the disappearing car right back to me. His eyes narrowed and his frown reappeared. "What did you get yourself into this time?"

*****

Thank you for reading!

I hope you enjoyed my book. I would really appreciate it if you'd leave a review on Amazon and Goodreads. Even a sentence or two would help.

Then turn the page to learn more about *Serf and Turf*, Book 3 in the Silicon Valley Mystery series.

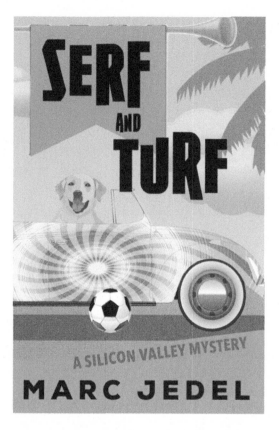

Follow the continuing adventures of Uncle Marty in *Serf and Turf*, Book 3 of the *Silicon Valley Mystery* series.

Danger abounds, but nothing may be harder for Marty than surviving a stay at his apartment by Buddy and young Megan. *Serf and Turf* starts the morning after Chutes and Ladder ends.

Get the first chapter free by joining my mailing list at:
www.marcjedel.com

Acknowledgements

Lots of love to my wife for her love, support, and willingness to brainstorm, review, and edit—even when she was tired. Love also to my kids, sister, father, and other family for their encouragement and support.

Special thanks to my beta and launch team who were so helpful with ideas, improvements, feedback, and support, especially Sandy, Bill, Linda, Jim, Fern, Laurie, Sherry, and Wendy. Thanks to Rick, Sharon, and Rebecca for inspiring Samantha's character, favorite baseball team, and fleshing out her personality. Thanks to Scott and Michelle for their hysterical stories about Bailey, which were only slightly exaggerated in the creation of Buddy.

Thanks to Kristen Weber for her key editorial feedback and for laughing at Marty. Thanks to Cara Quinlan for her copy-editing that made my writing better. And thanks to Keri Knutson for her beautiful covers.

Even though I still don't like camping, please support your local Girl Scout troop.

About the Author

For most of my life, I've been inventing stories. Some, especially when I was young, involved my sister as the villain. As my sister's brother for her entire life, I'm highly qualified to tell the tale of this evolving, quirky sibling relationship.

The publication of my first novel, *Uncle and Ants*, gave me permission to claim "author" as my job. This leads to much more interesting conversations than answering, "marketing." Although, I have my years of marketing leadership positions in Silicon Valley to thank for honing my writing skills. While my high-tech marketing roles involved crafting plenty of fiction, we called these marketing collateral, emails, and ads.

My family would tell you that Marty's character isn't much of a stretch of the imagination for me, but I proudly resemble that remark. Like Marty, I live in Silicon Valley and can't believe that normal people would willingly jump out of an airplane. Unlike Marty, I have a wonderful wife and a neurotic but sweet small dog who is often the first to weigh in on the humor in my writing.

Thanks for reading *Chutes and Ladder*! Visit www.marcjedel.com for more.

— Marc

Made in the USA
Coppell, TX
26 December 2022

90778450R00125